Pea, Bee, & Jay
WANNABEES

Brian "Smitty" Smith

HARPER
alley

An Imprint of HarperCollins Publishers

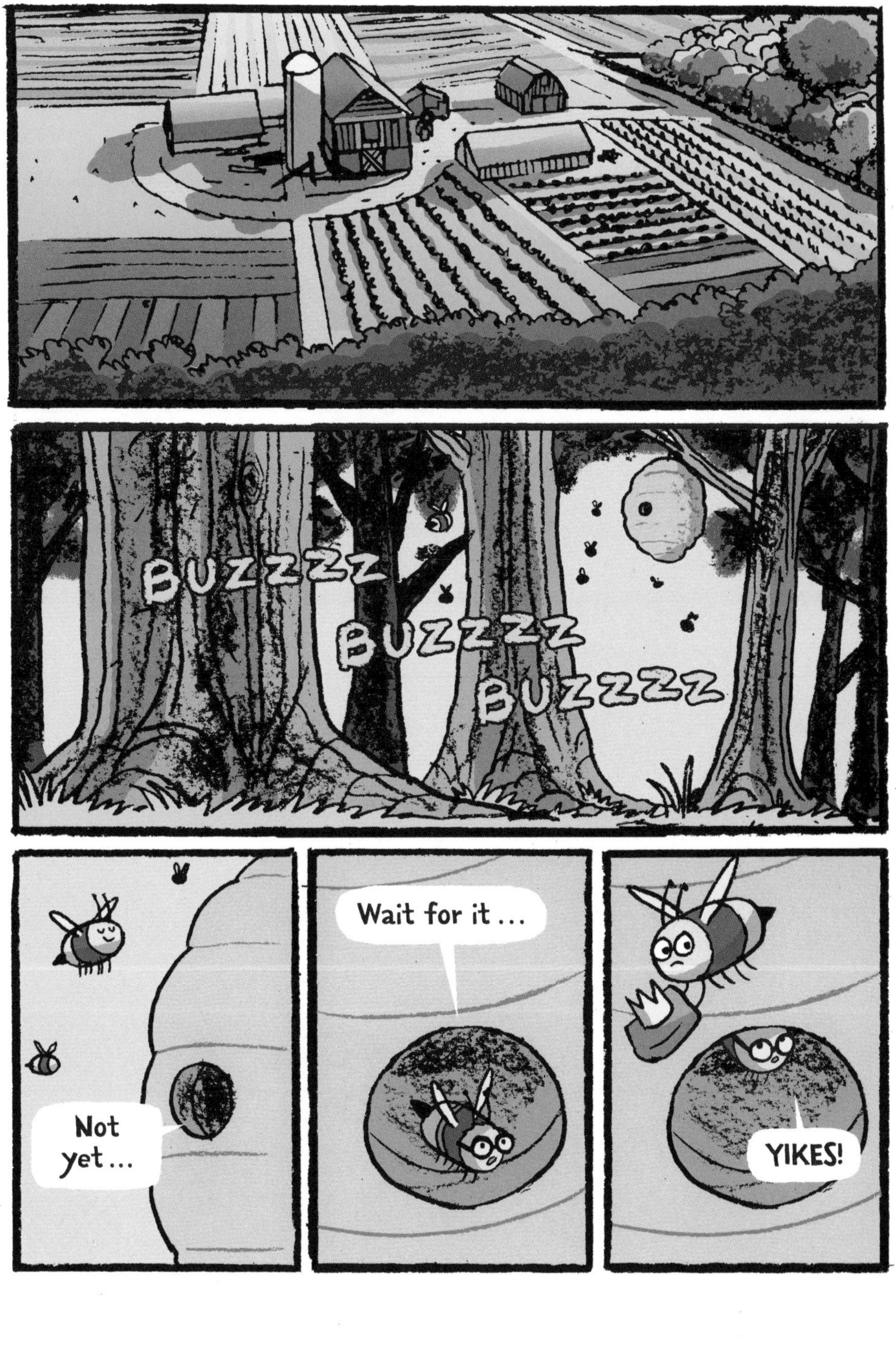
BUZZZZZ
BUZZZZZ
BUZZZZZ
Not yet...
Wait for it...
YIKES!

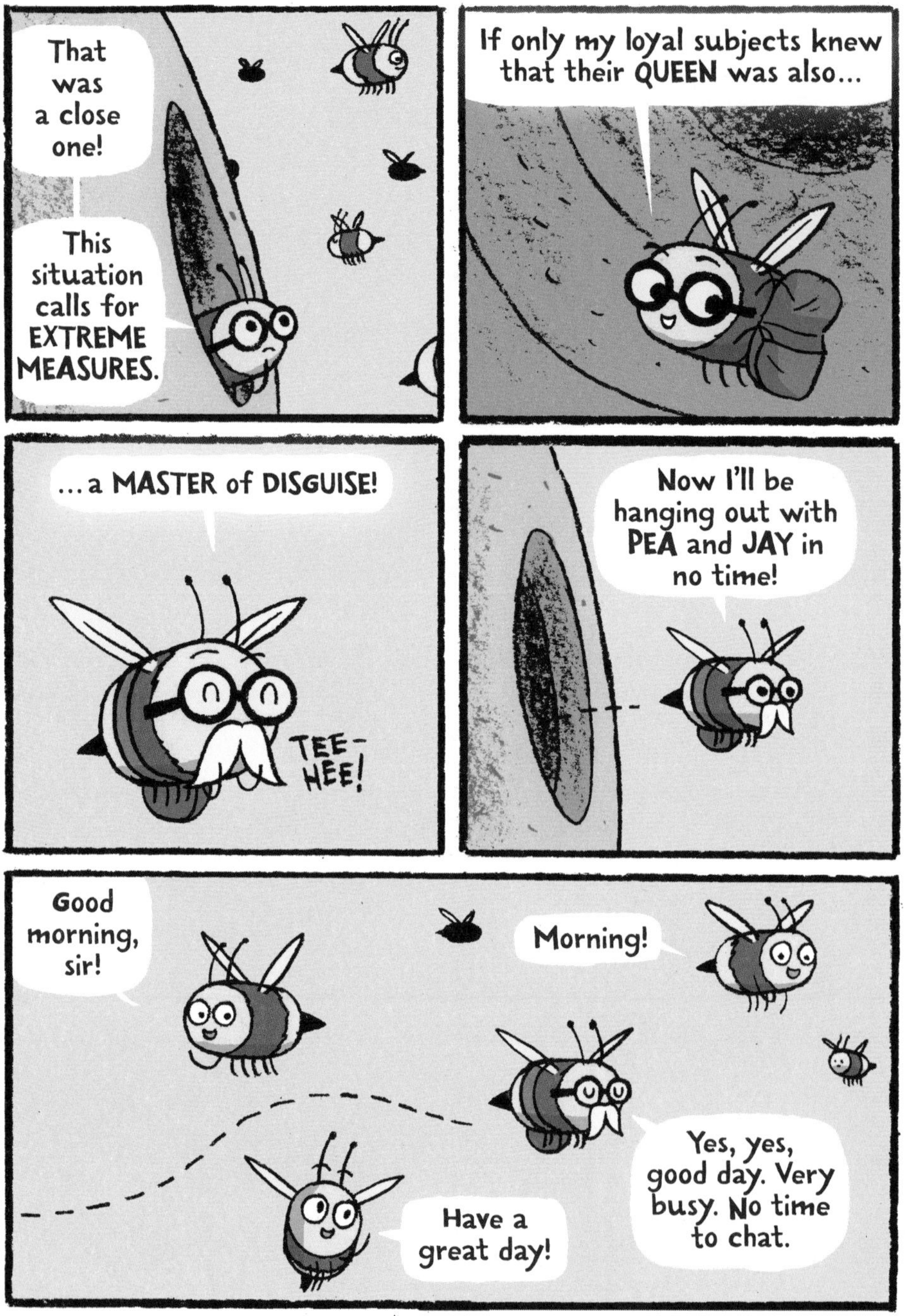
That was a close one!
This situation calls for EXTREME MEASURES.
If only my loyal subjects knew that their QUEEN was also...
...a MASTER of DISGUISE!
TEE-HEE!
Now I'll be hanging out with PEA and JAY in no time!
Good morning, sir!
Morning!
Yes, yes, good day. Very busy. No time to chat.
Have a great day!

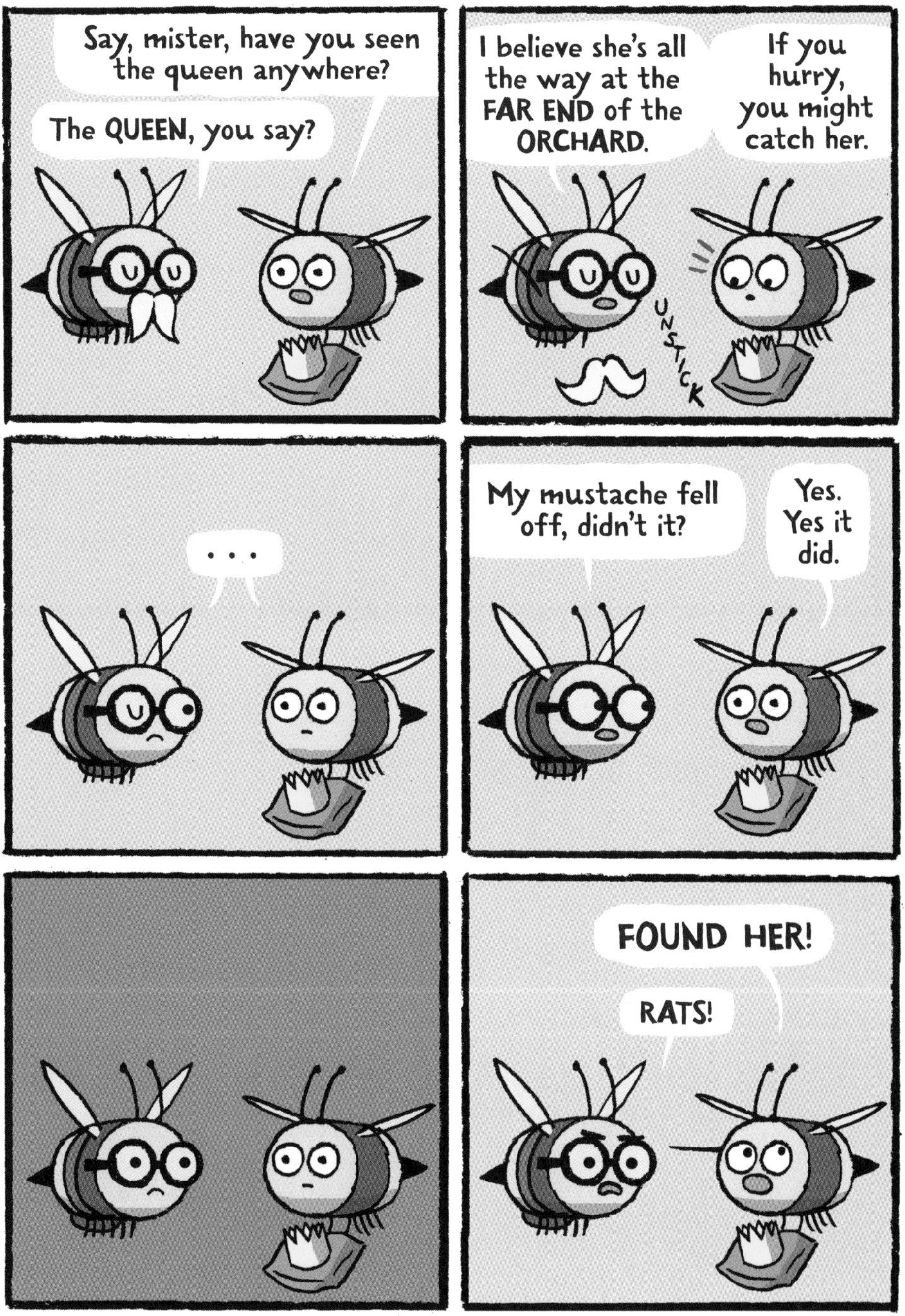
Say, mister, have you seen the queen anywhere?
The QUEEN, you say?
I believe she's all the way at the FAR END of the ORCHARD.
If you hurry, you might catch her.
UNSTICK
. . .
My mustache fell off, didn't it?
Yes. Yes it did.
FOUND HER!
RATS!

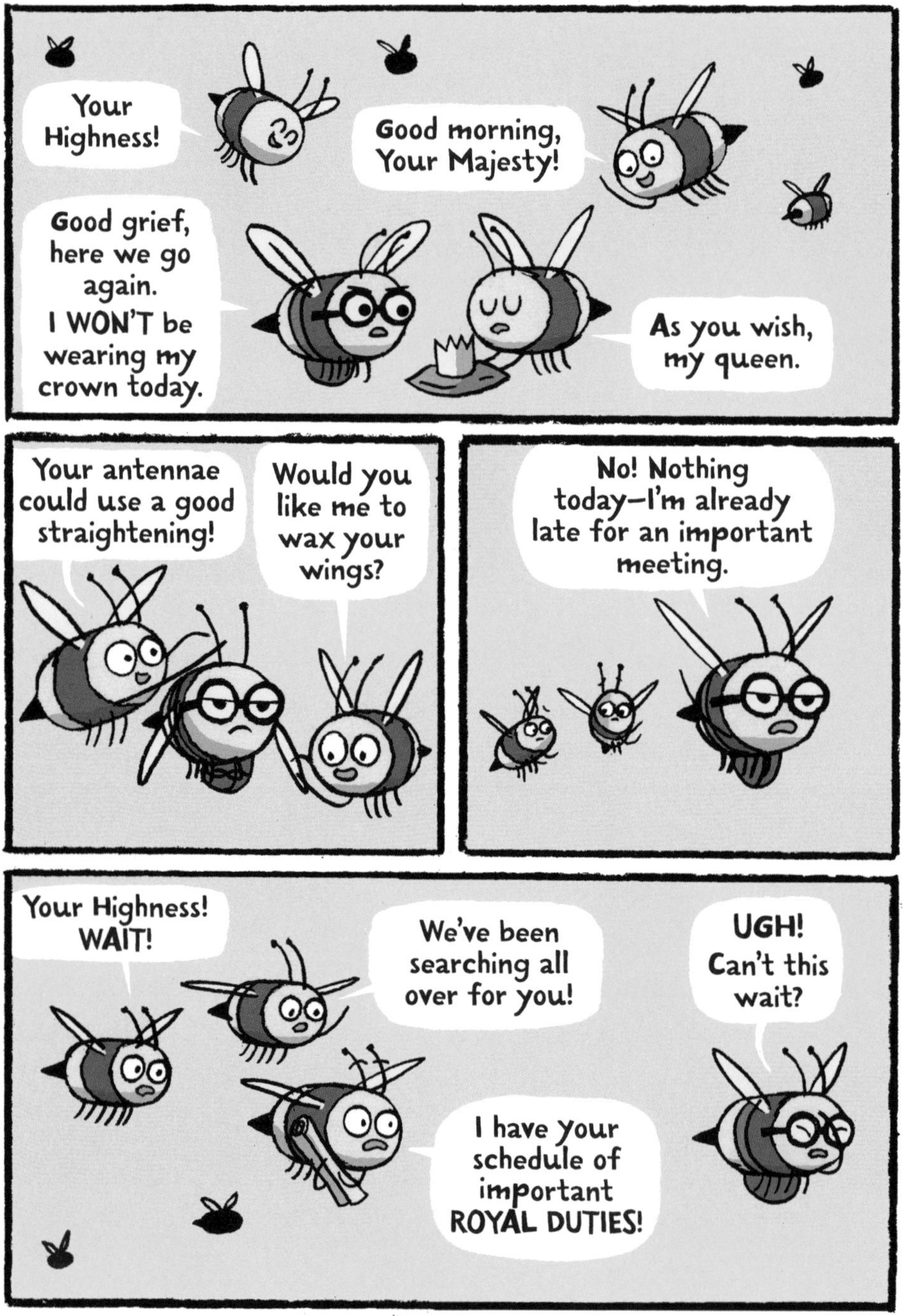
Your Highness!
Good morning, Your Majesty!
Good grief, here we go again. I WON'T be wearing my crown today.
As you wish, my queen.
Your antennae could use a good straightening!
Would you like me to wax your wings?
No! Nothing today—I'm already late for an important meeting.
Your Highness! WAIT!
We've been searching all over for you!
UGH! Can't this wait?
I have your schedule of important ROYAL DUTIES!

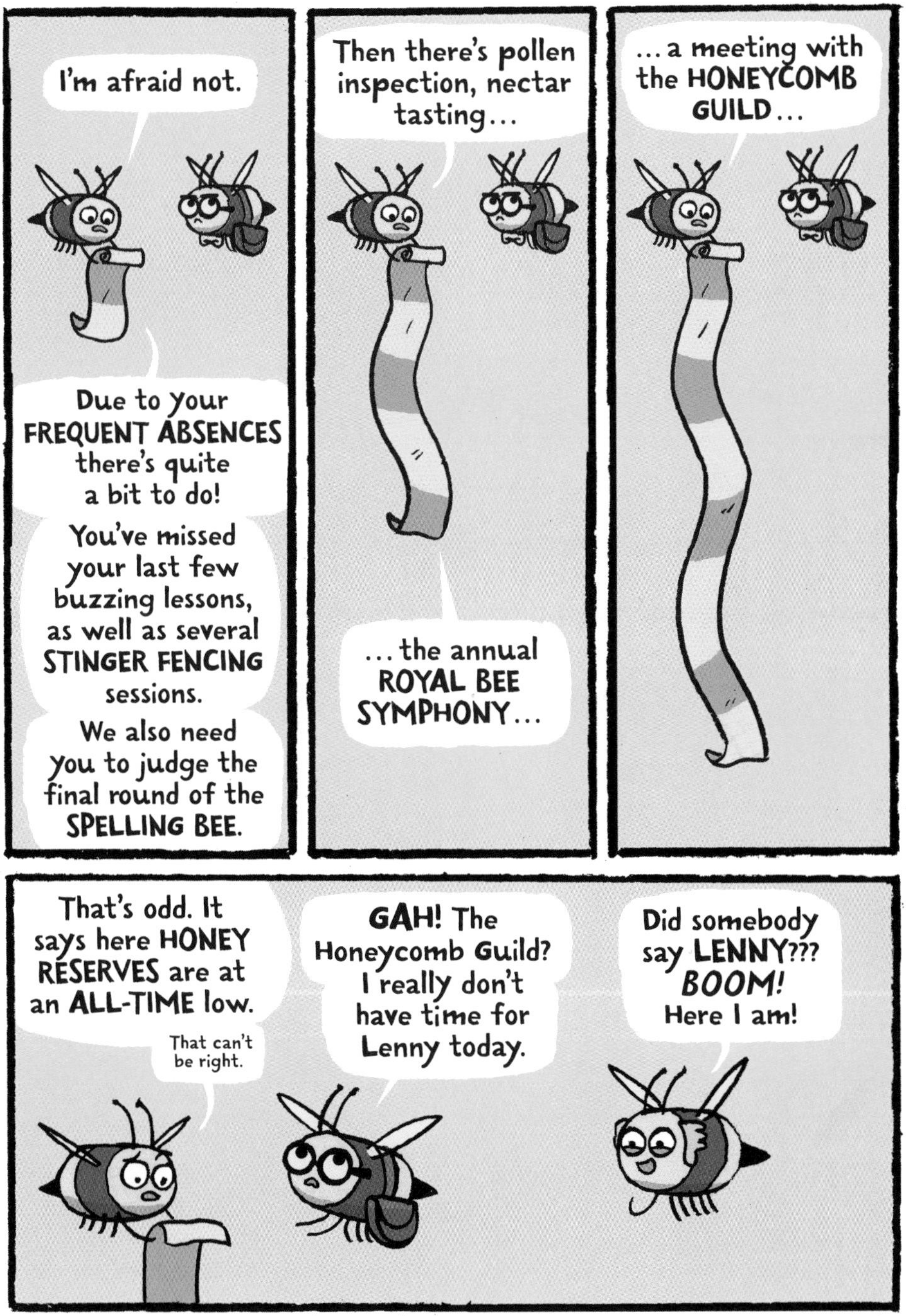
I'm afraid not.
Due to your FREQUENT ABSENCES there's quite a bit to do!
You've missed your last few buzzing lessons, as well as several STINGER FENCING sessions.
We also need you to judge the final round of the SPELLING BEE.
Then there's pollen inspection, nectar tasting...
... the annual ROYAL BEE SYMPHONY...
... a meeting with the HONEYCOMB GUILD...
That's odd. It says here HONEY RESERVES are at an ALL-TIME low.
That can't be right.
GAH! The Honeycomb Guild? I really don't have time for Lenny today.
Did somebody say LENNY??? BOOM! Here I am!

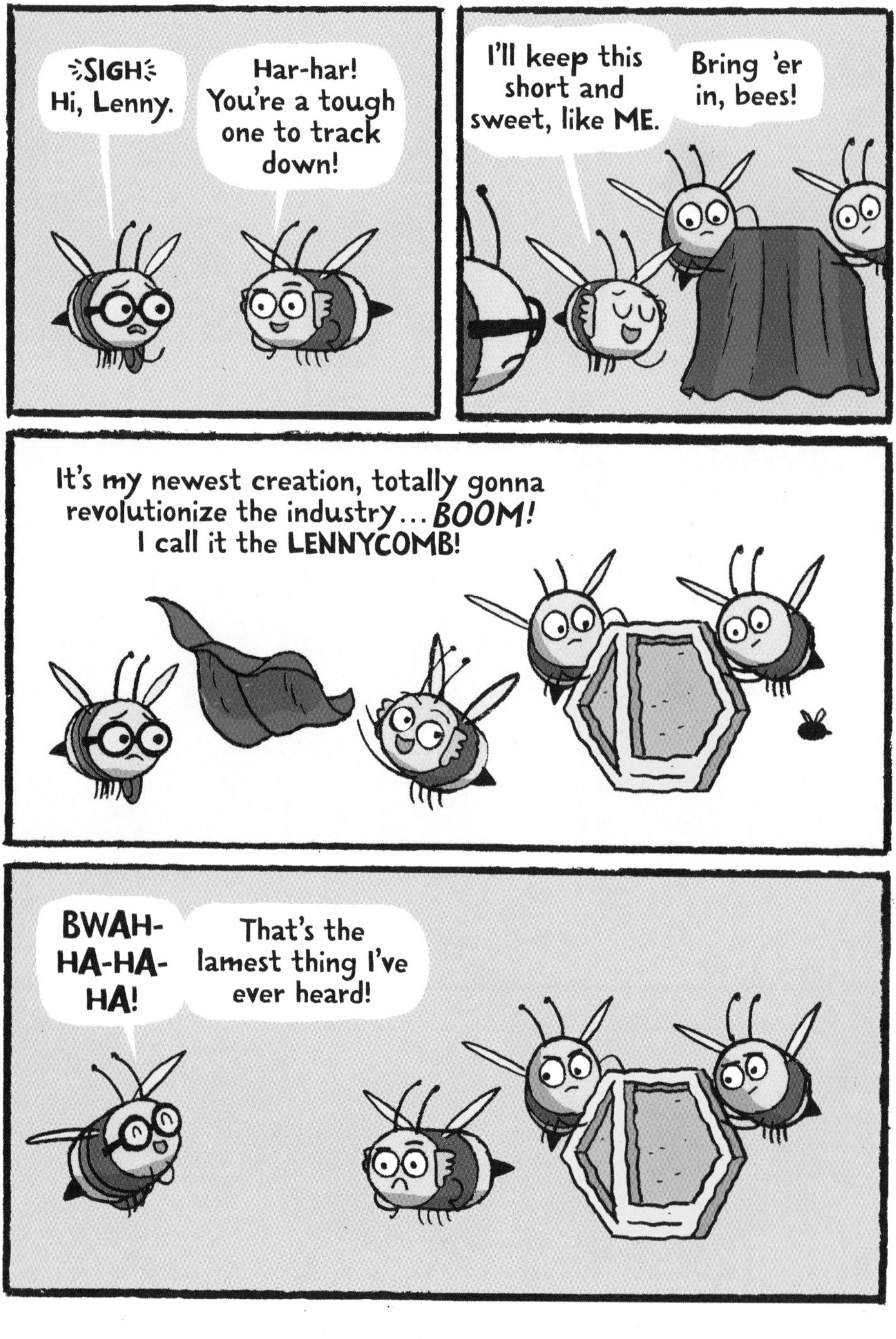
SIGH
Hi, Lenny.
Har-har! You're a tough one to track down!
I'll keep this short and sweet, like ME.
Bring 'er in, bees!
It's my newest creation, totally gonna revolutionize the industry... BOOM! I call it the LENNYCOMB!
BWAH-HA-HA-HA!
That's the lamest thing I've ever heard!

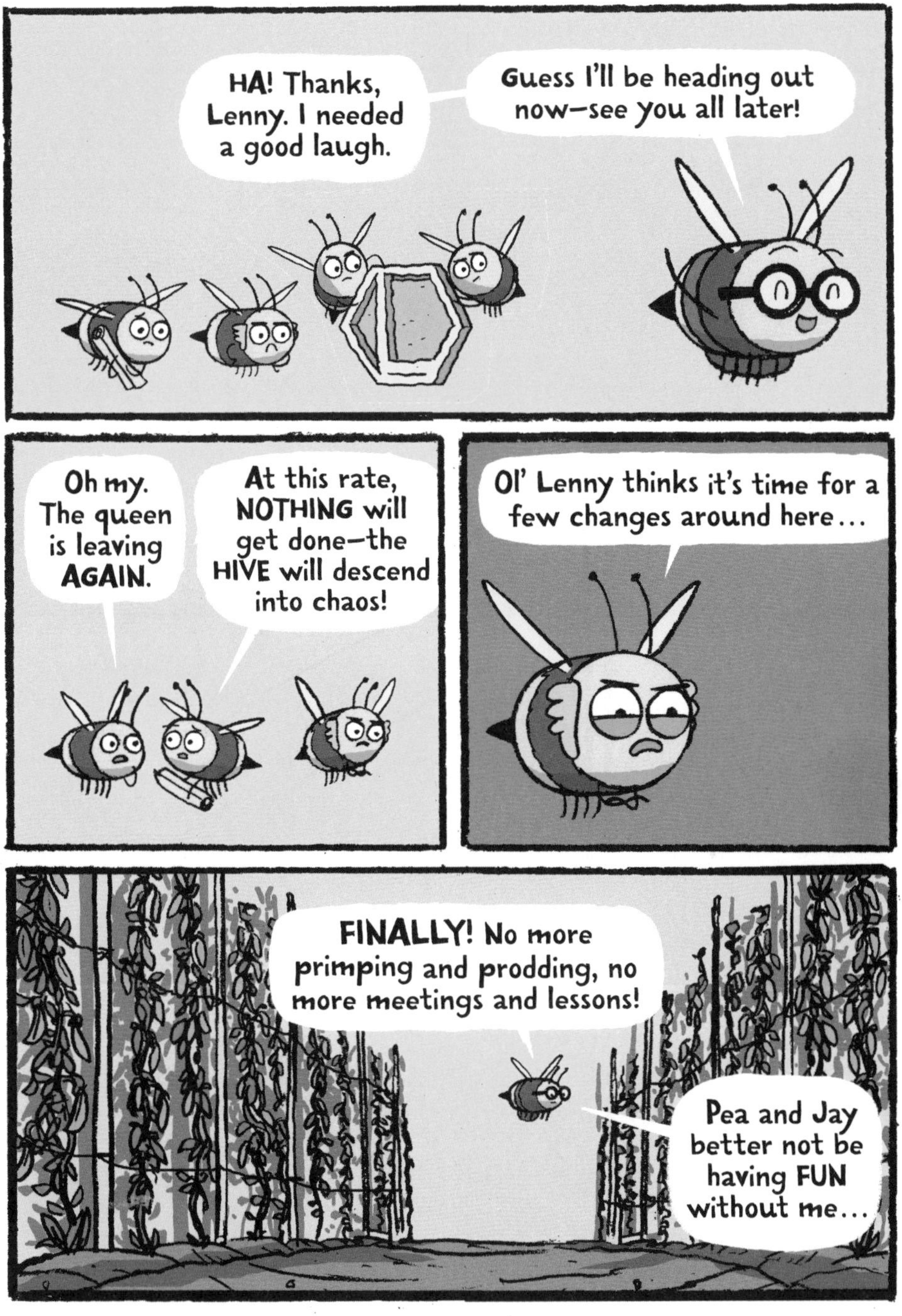
HA! Thanks, Lenny. I needed a good laugh.
Guess I'll be heading out now—see you all later!
Oh my. The queen is leaving AGAIN.
At this rate, NOTHING will get done—the HIVE will descend into chaos!
Ol' Lenny thinks it's time for a few changes around here…
FINALLY! No more primping and prodding, no more meetings and lessons!
Pea and Jay better not be having FUN without me…

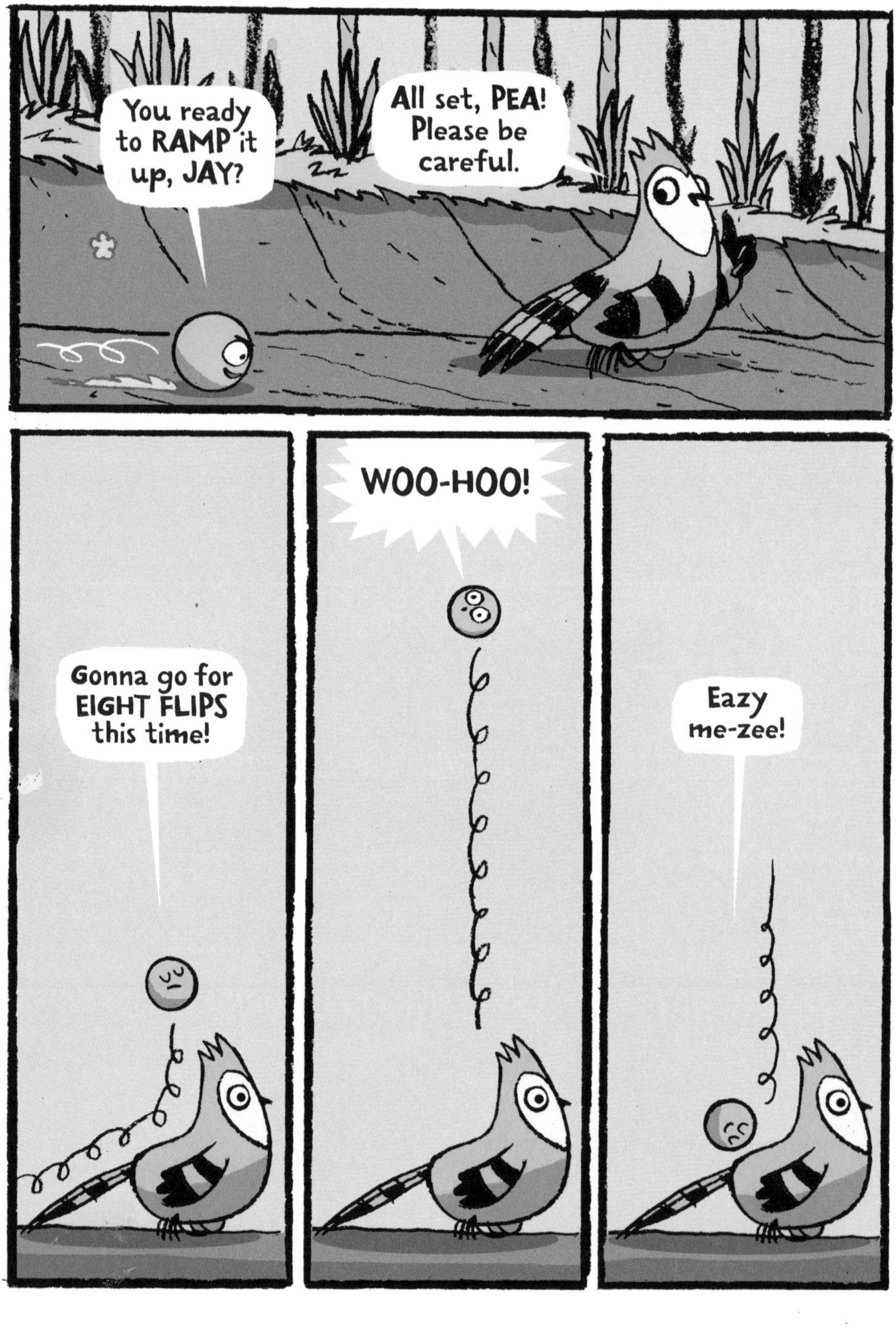
You ready to RAMP it up, JAY?
All set, PEA! Please be careful.
Gonna go for EIGHT FLIPS this time!
WOO-HOO!
Eazy me-zee!

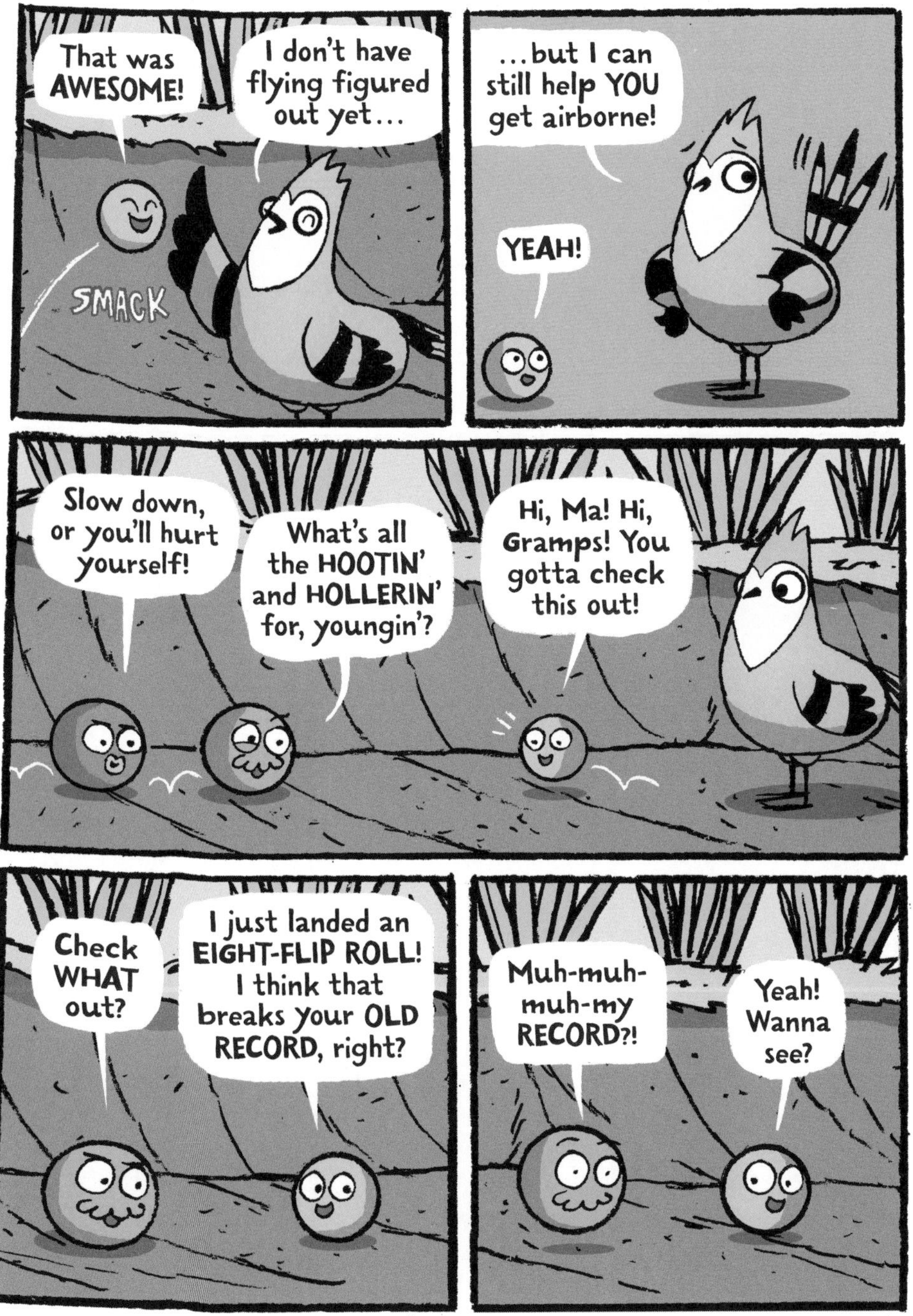
That was AWESOME!
SMACK
I don't have flying figured out yet...
...but I can still help YOU get airborne!
YEAH!
Slow down, or you'll hurt yourself!
What's all the HOOTIN' and HOLLERIN' for, youngin'?
Hi, Ma! Hi, Gramps! You gotta check this out!
Check WHAT out?
I just landed an EIGHT-FLIP ROLL! I think that breaks your OLD RECORD, right?
Muh-muh-muh-my RECORD?!
Yeah! Wanna see?

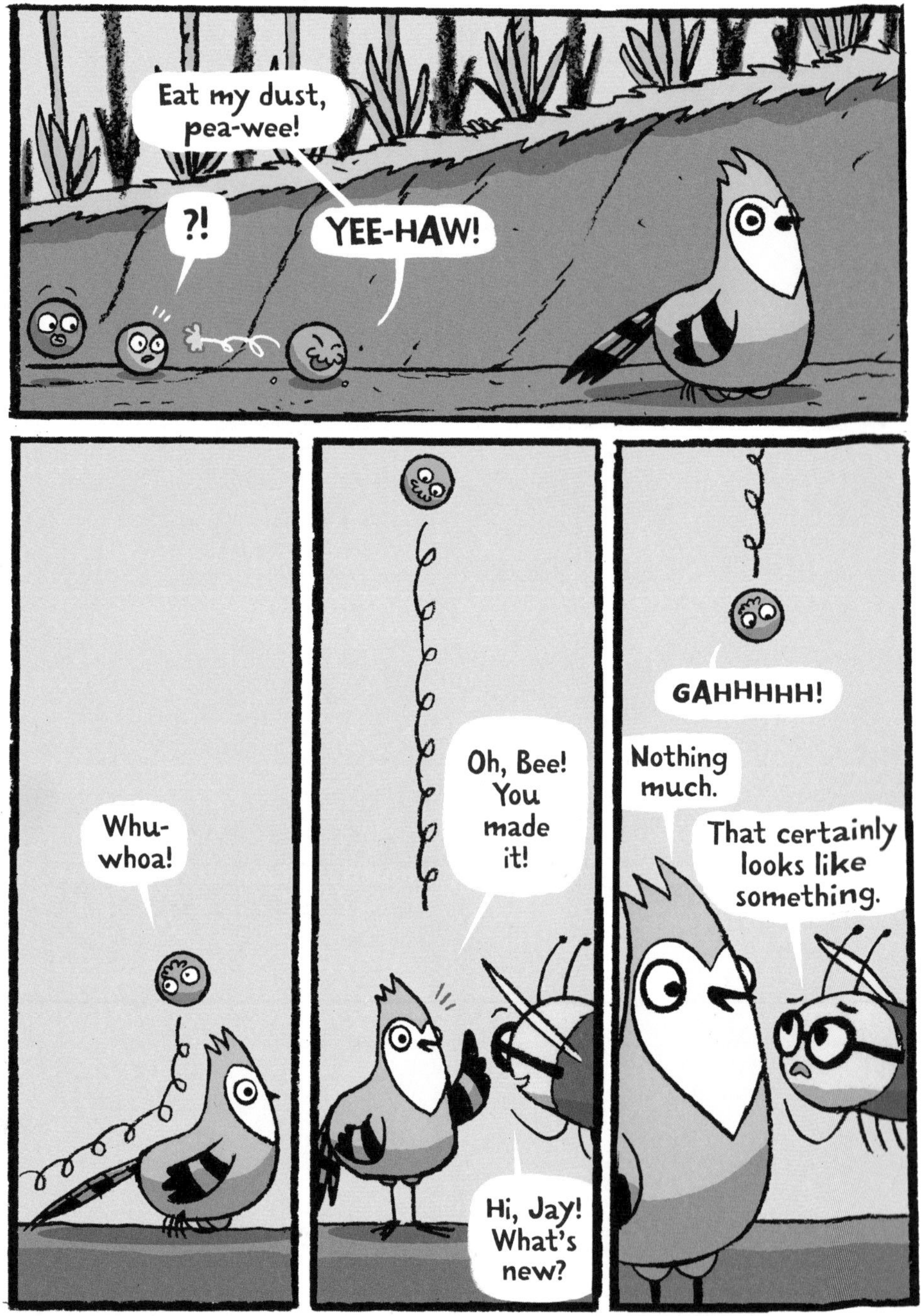
Eat my dust, pea-wee!
?!
YEE-HAW!
Whu-whoa!
Oh, Bee! You made it!
Hi, Jay! What's new?
GAHHHHH!
Nothing much.
That certainly looks like something.

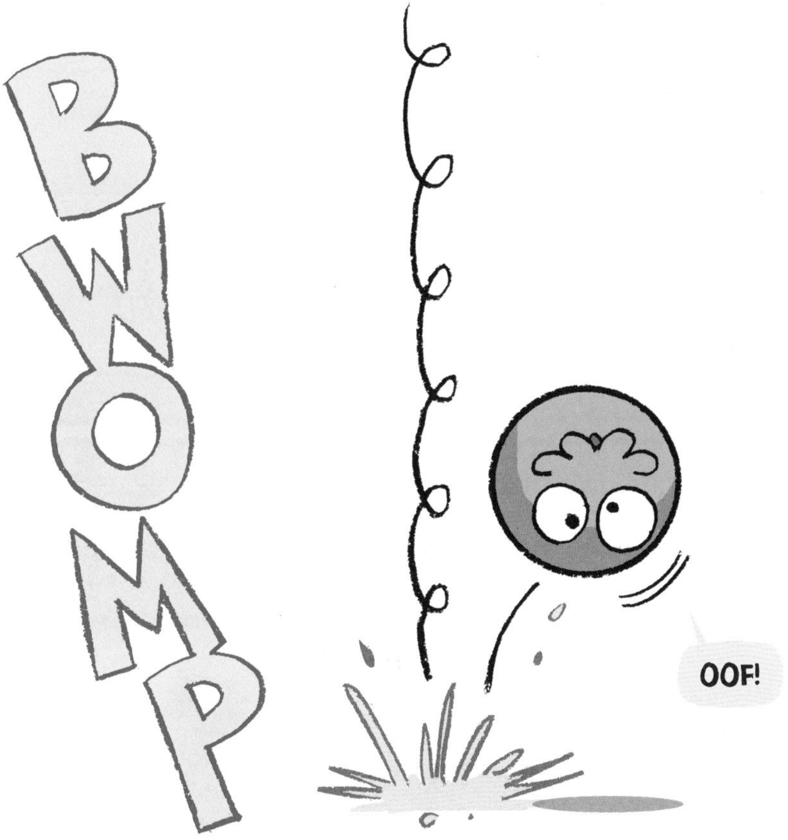
BWOMP
OOF!

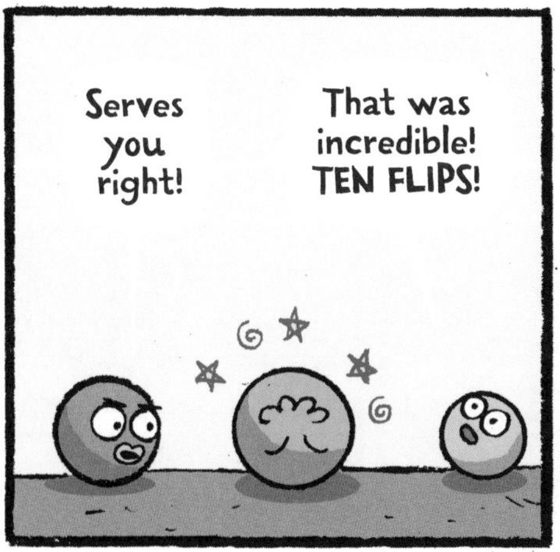
Serves you right!
That was incredible! TEN FLIPS!

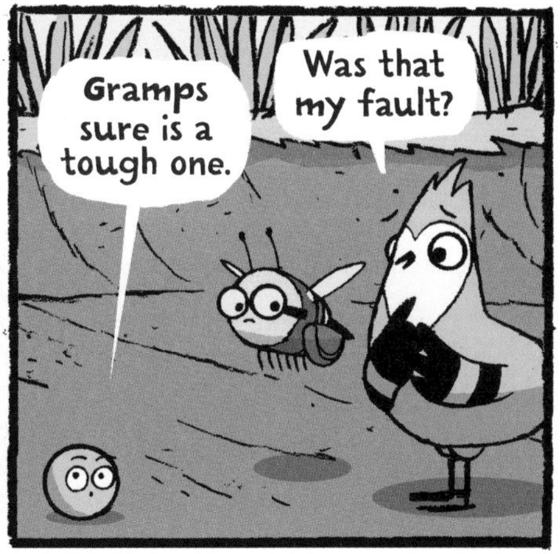
Gramps sure is a tough one.
Was that my fault?

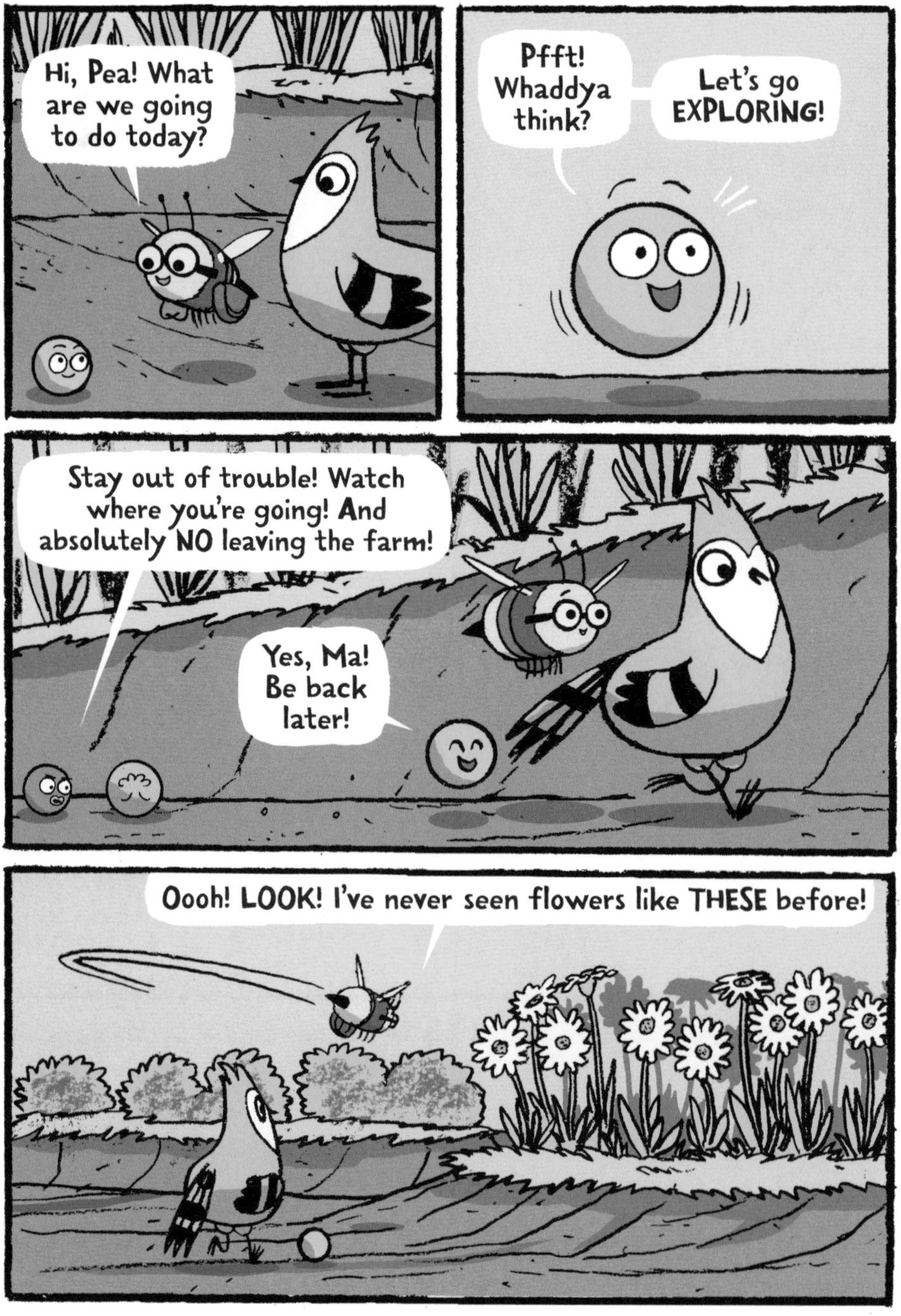
Hi, Pea! What are we going to do today?
Pfft! Whaddya think?
Let's go EXPLORING!
Stay out of trouble! Watch where you're going! And absolutely NO leaving the farm!
Yes, Ma! Be back later!
Oooh! LOOK! I've never seen flowers like THESE before!

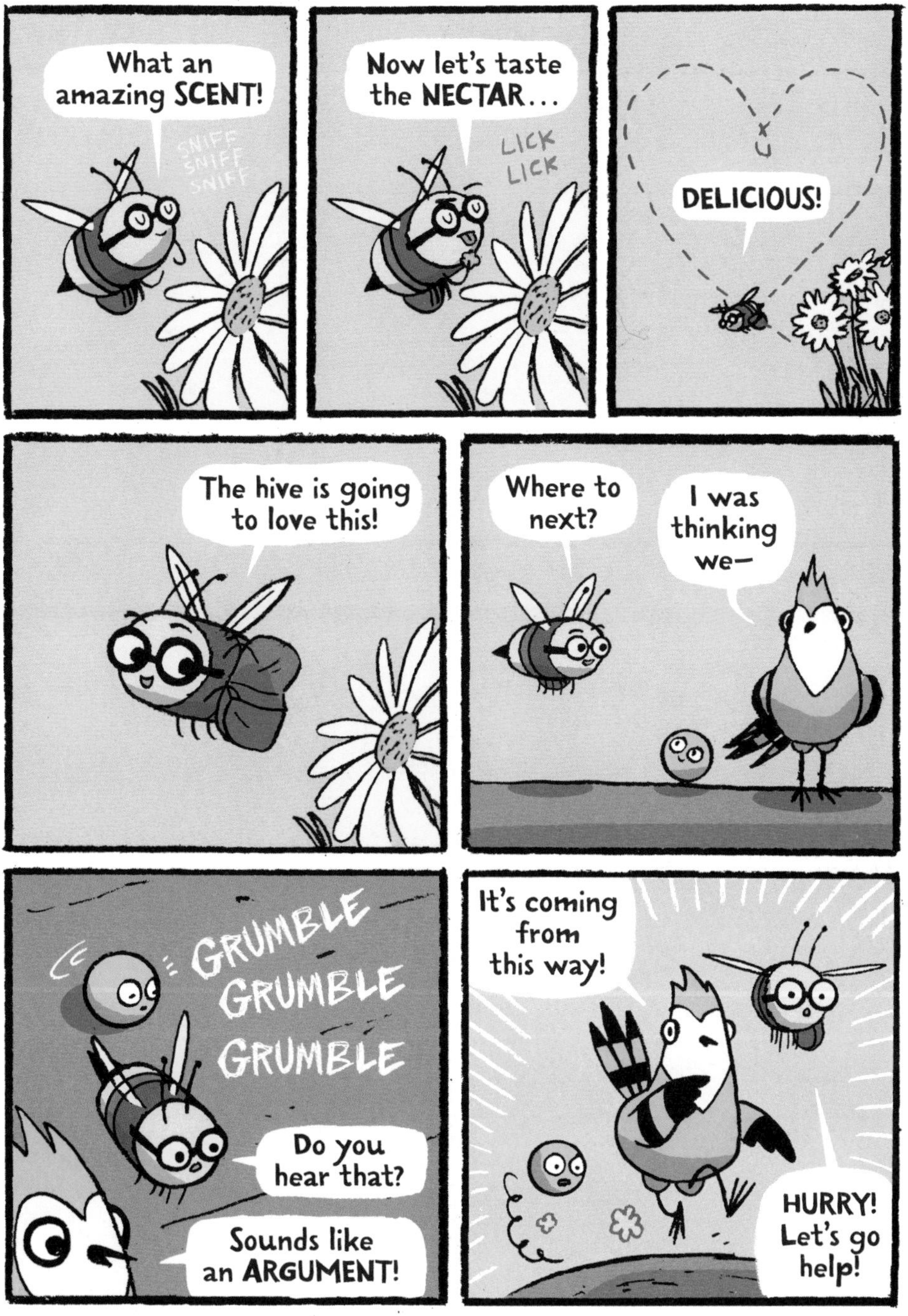
What an amazing SCENT!
SNIFF SNIFF SNIFF
Now let's taste the NECTAR...
LICK LICK
DELICIOUS!
The hive is going to love this!
Where to next?
I was thinking we—
GRUMBLE GRUMBLE GRUMBLE
Do you hear that?
Sounds like an ARGUMENT!
It's coming from this way!
HURRY! Let's go help!

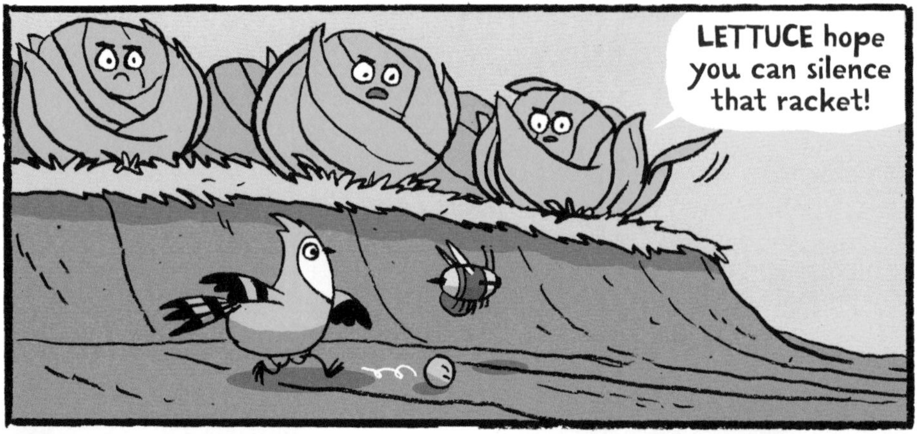
LETTUCE hope you can silence that racket!

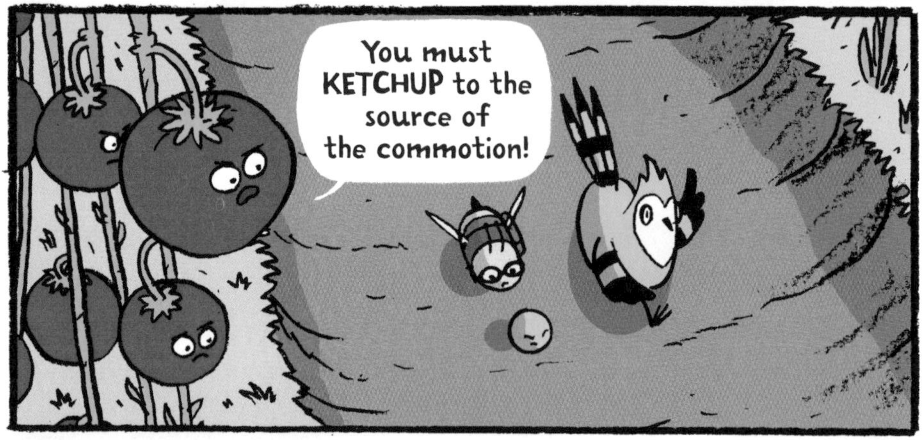
You must KETCHUP to the source of the commotion!

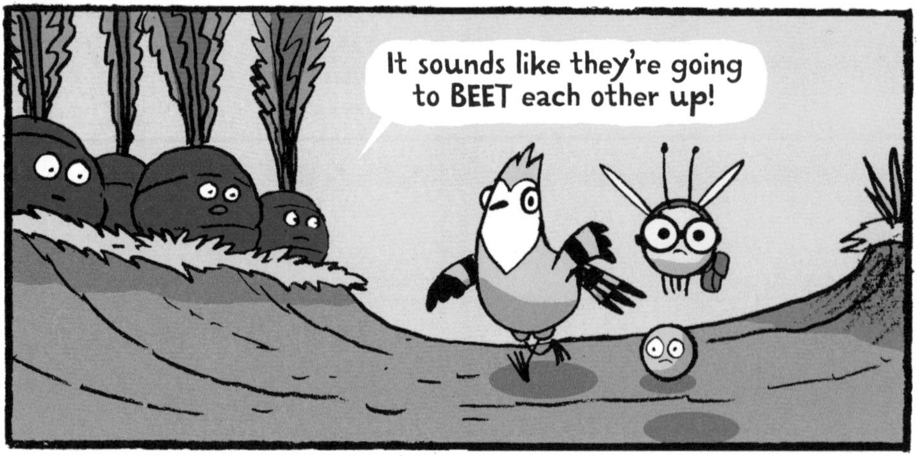
It sounds like they're going to BEET each other up!

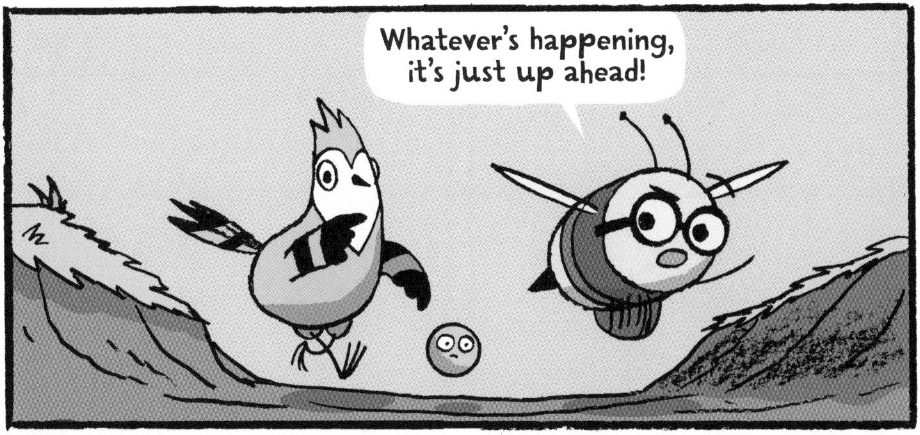
Whatever's happening, it's just up ahead!

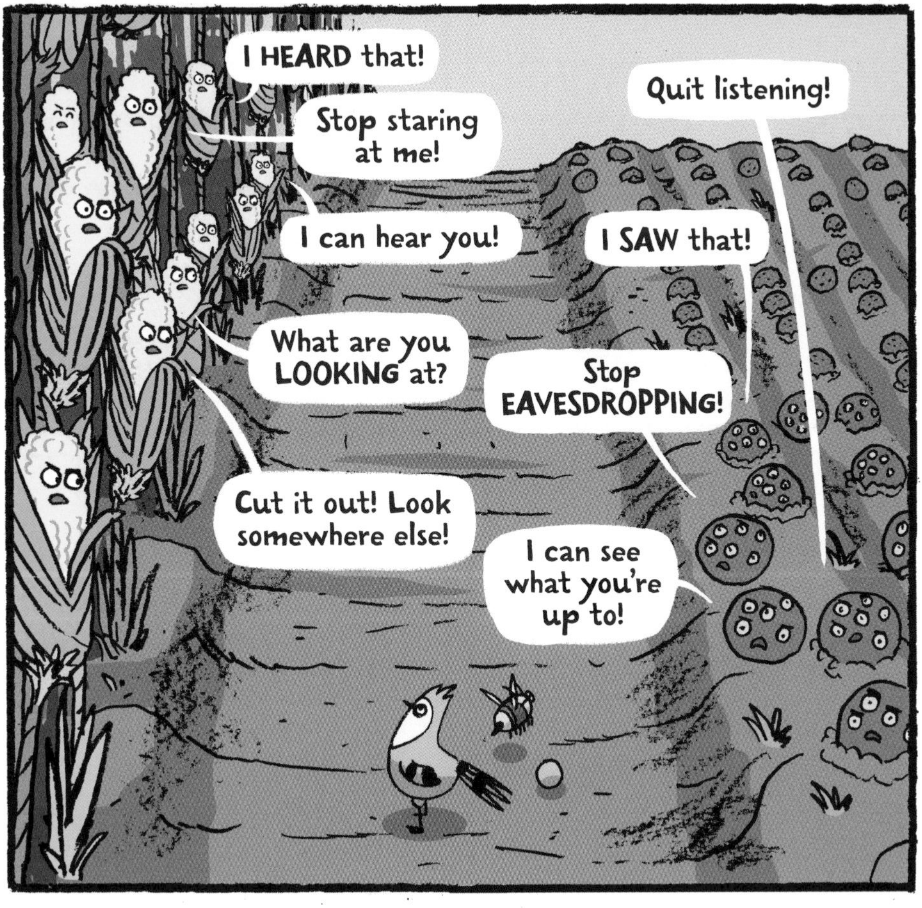
I HEARD that!
Stop staring at me!
I can hear you!
What are you LOOKING at?
Cut it out! Look somewhere else!
Quit listening!
I SAW that!
Stop EAVESDROPPING!
I can see what you're up to!

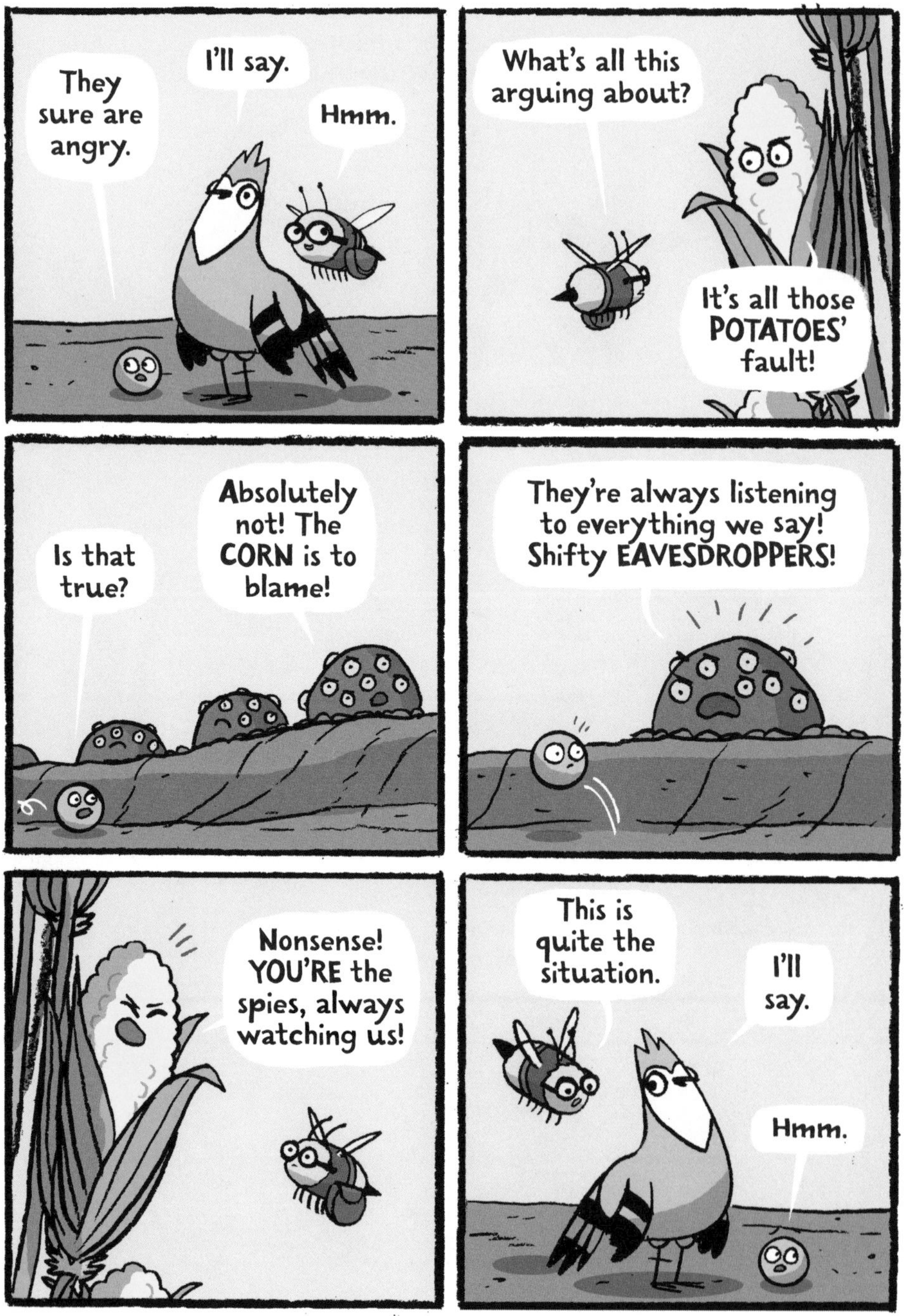
They sure are angry.
I'll say.
Hmm.
What's all this arguing about?
It's all those POTATOES' fault!
Is that true?
Absolutely not! The CORN is to blame!
They're always listening to everything we say! Shifty EAVESDROPPERS!
Nonsense! YOU'RE the spies, always watching us!
This is quite the situation.
I'll say.
Hmm.

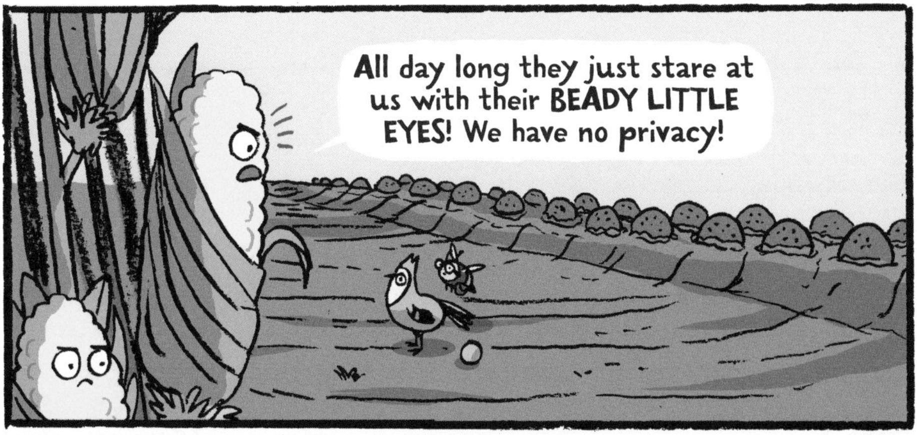
All day long they just stare at us with their BEADY LITTLE EYES! We have no privacy!

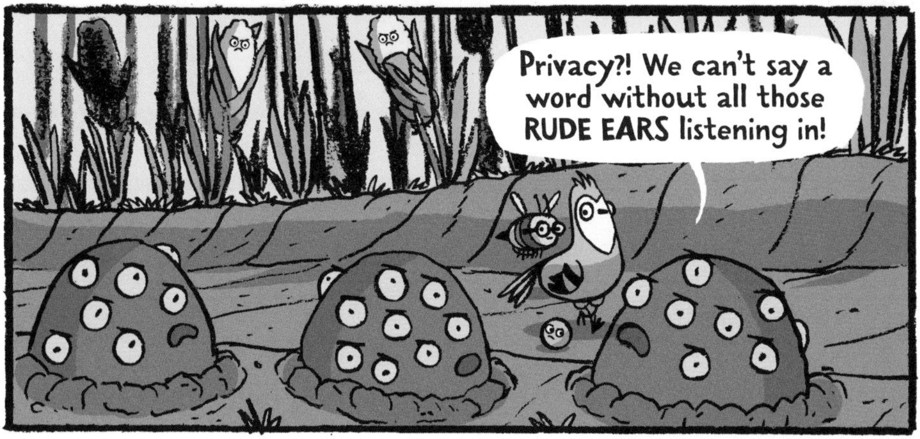
Privacy?! We can't say a word without all those RUDE EARS listening in!

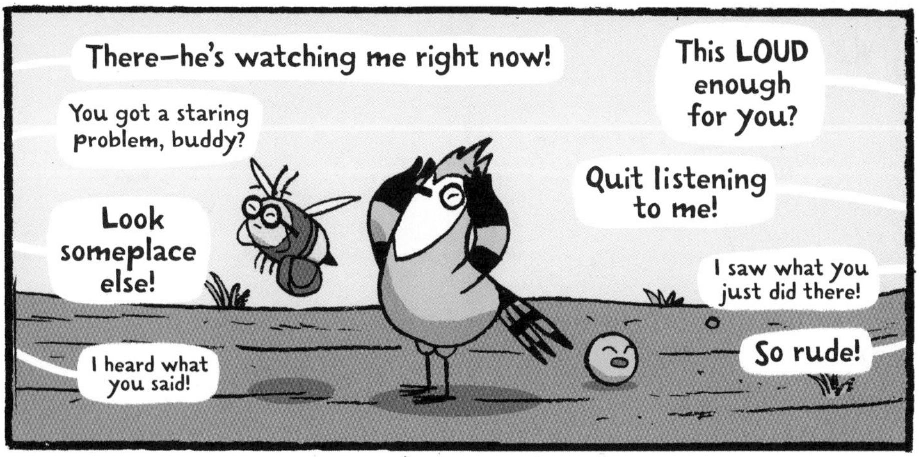
There—he's watching me right now!
This LOUD enough for you?
You got a staring problem, buddy?
Quit listening to me!
Look someplace else!
I saw what you just did there!
So rude!
I heard what you said!

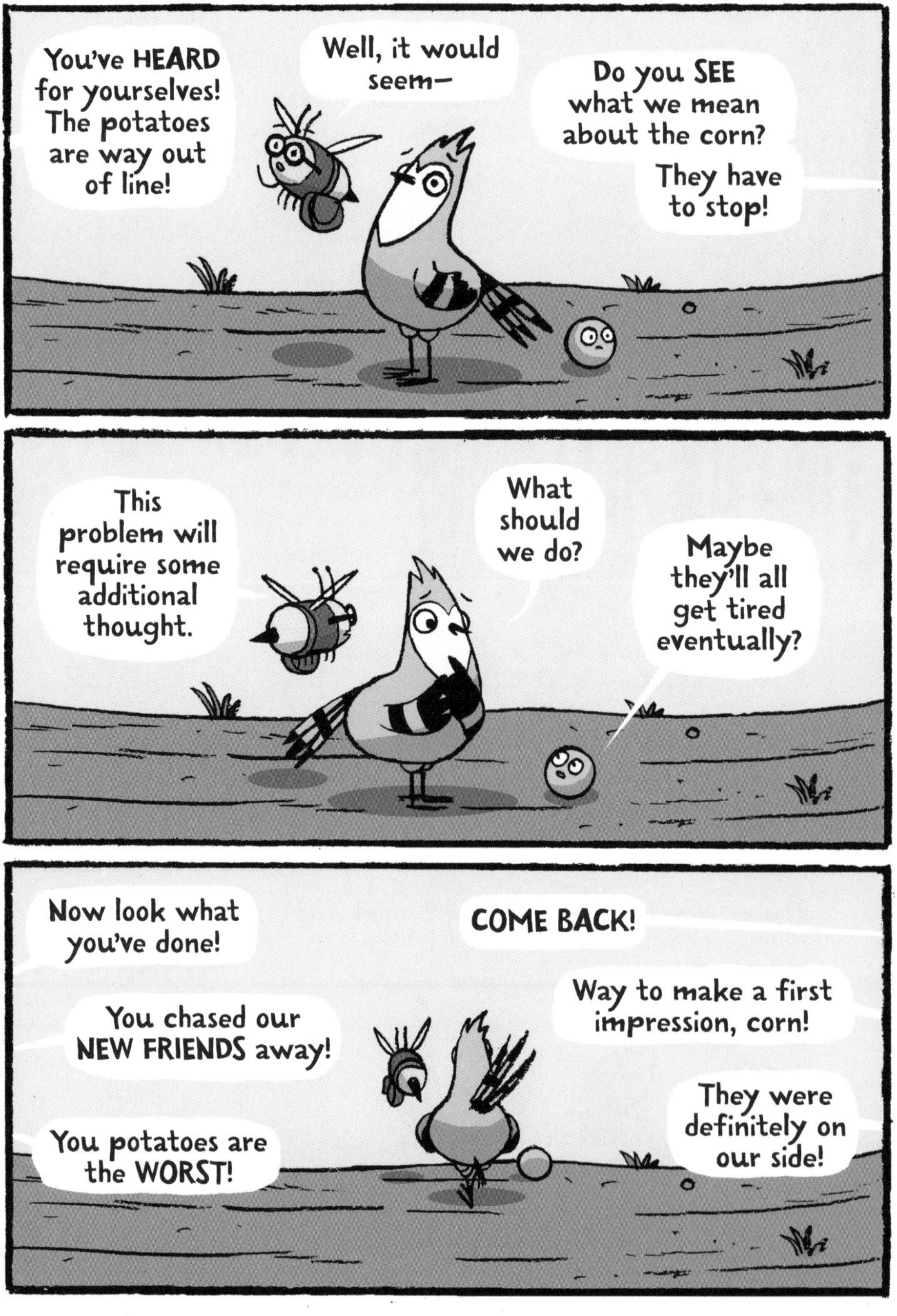
You've HEARD for yourselves! The potatoes are way out of line!
Well, it would seem—
Do you SEE what we mean about the corn?
They have to stop!
This problem will require some additional thought.
What should we do?
Maybe they'll all get tired eventually?
Now look what you've done!
You chased our NEW FRIENDS away!
You potatoes are the WORST!
COME BACK!
Way to make a first impression, corn!
They were definitely on our side!

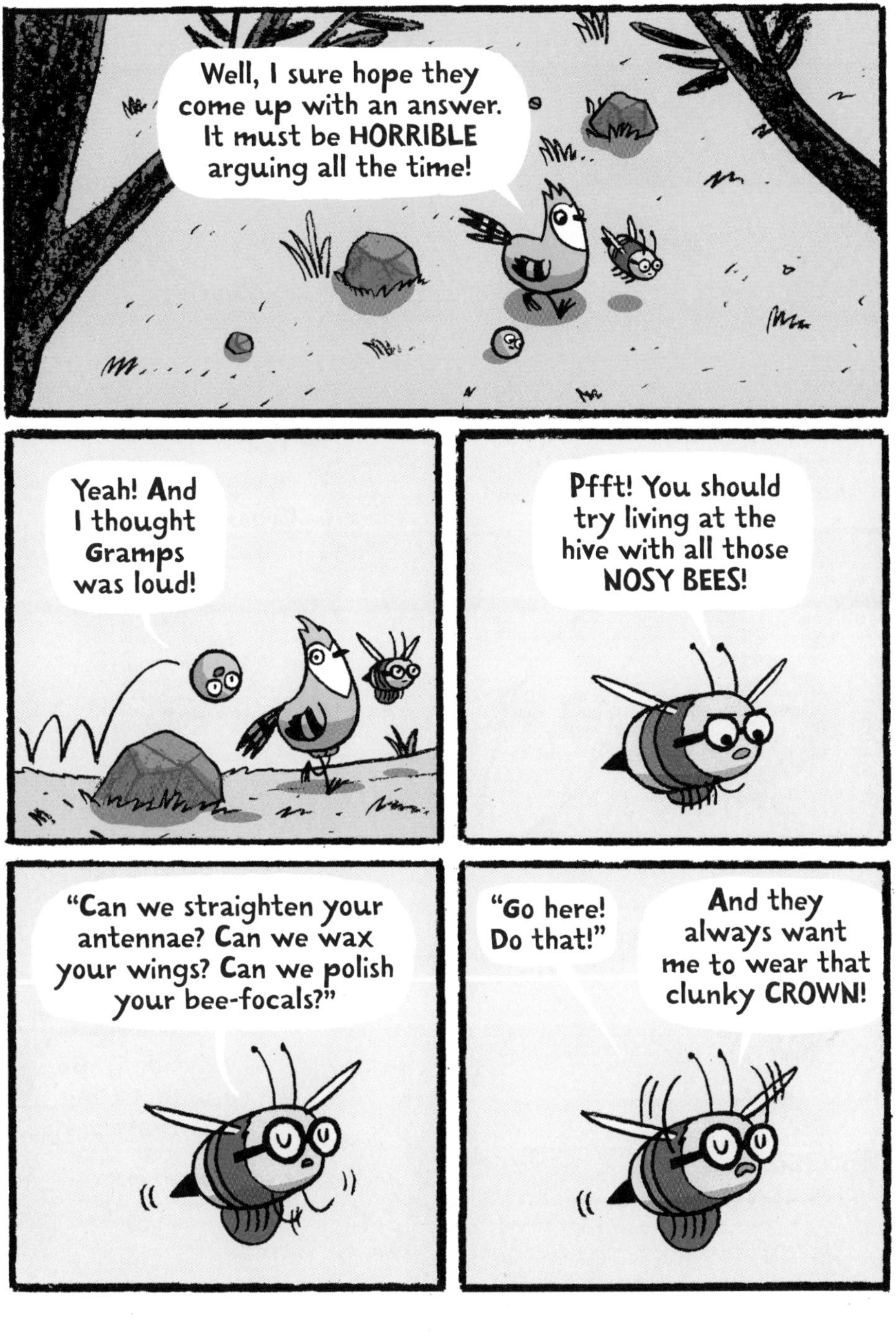
Well, I sure hope they come up with an answer. It must be HORRIBLE arguing all the time!
Yeah! And I thought Gramps was loud!
Pfft! You should try living at the hive with all those NOSY BEES!
"Can we straighten your antennae? Can we wax your wings? Can we polish your bee-focals?"
"Go here! Do that!"
And they always want me to wear that clunky CROWN!

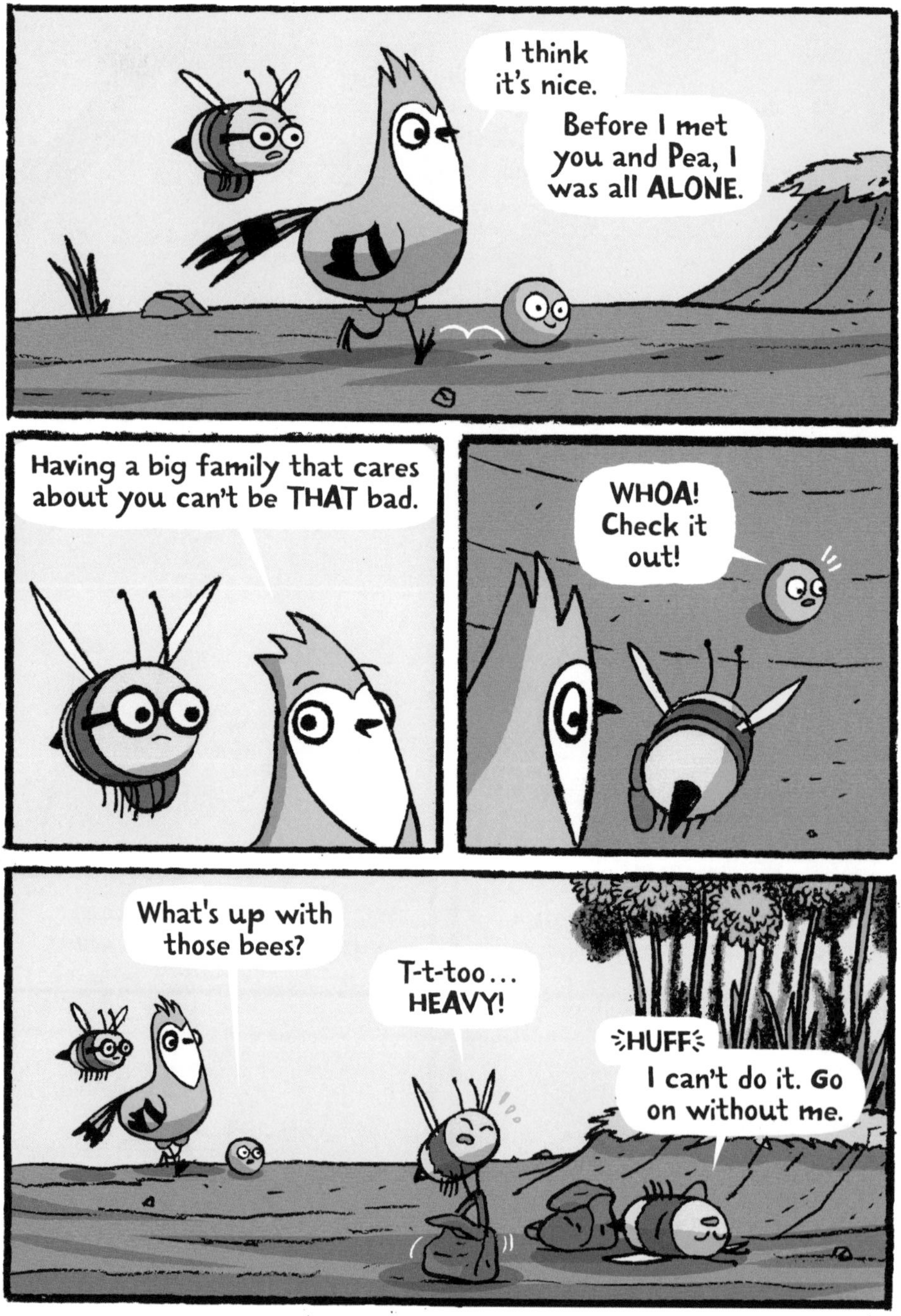

I think it's nice.
Before I met you and Pea, I was all ALONE.
Having a big family that cares about you can't be THAT bad.
WHOA! Check it out!
What's up with those bees?
T-t-too... HEAVY!
HUFF
I can't do it. Go on without me.

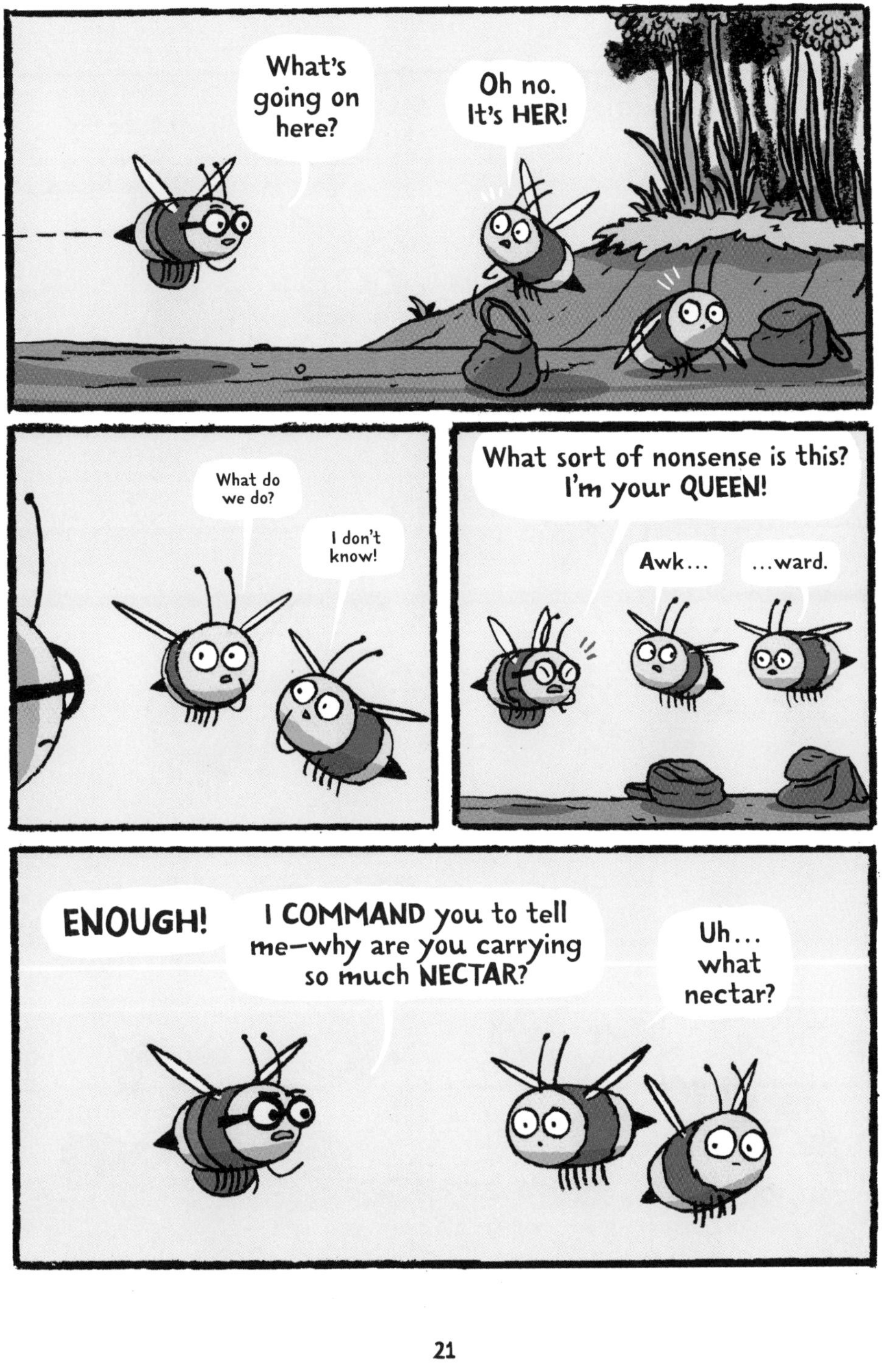

What's going on here?
Oh no. It's HER!
What do we do?
I don't know!
What sort of nonsense is this? I'm your QUEEN!
Awk...
...ward.
ENOUGH!
I COMMAND you to tell me—why are you carrying so much NECTAR?
Uh... what nectar?

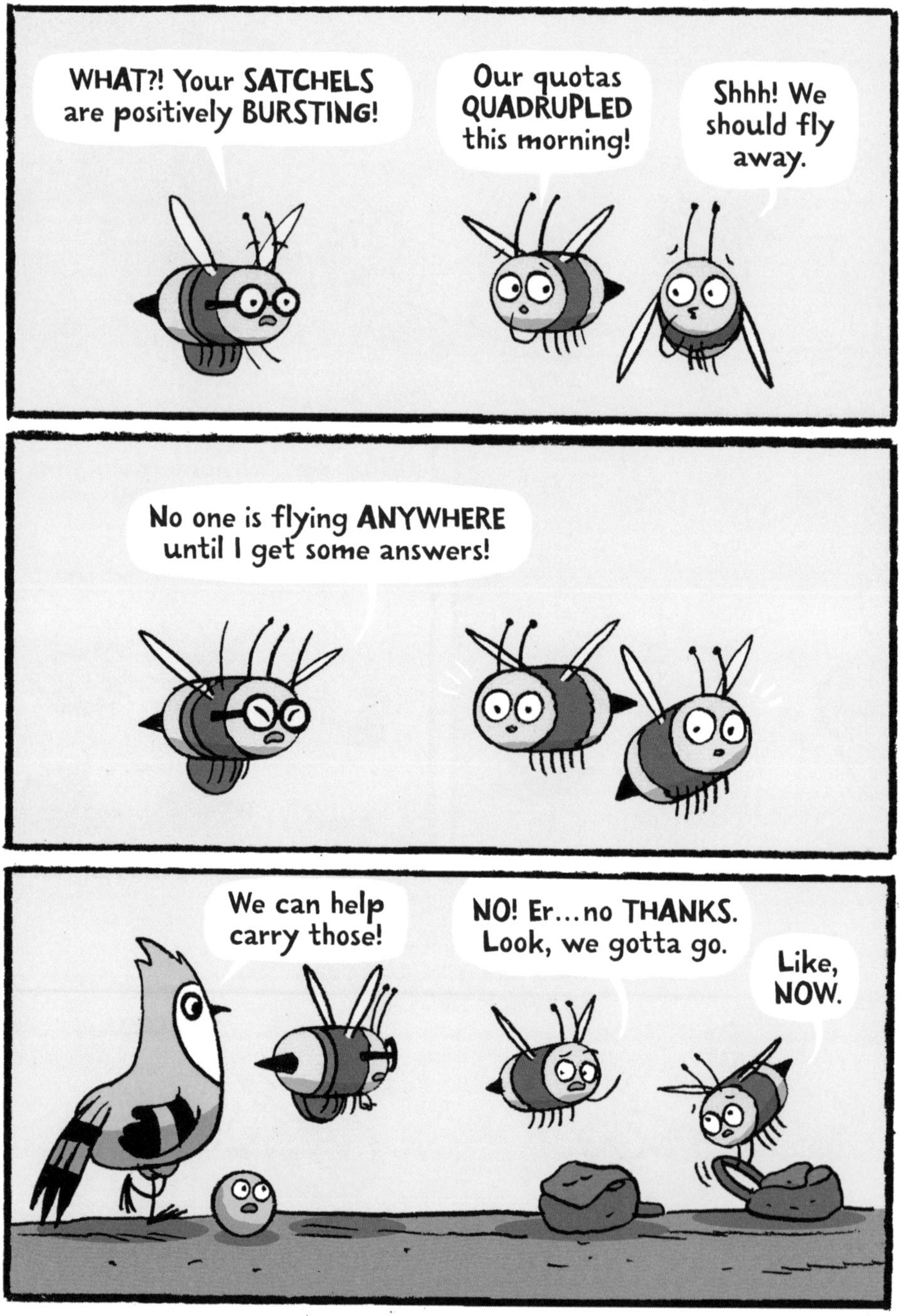
WHAT?! Your SATCHELS are positively BURSTING!
Our quotas QUADRUPLED this morning!
Shhh! We should fly away.
No one is flying ANYWHERE until I get some answers!
We can help carry those!
NO! Er...no THANKS. Look, we gotta go.
Like, NOW.

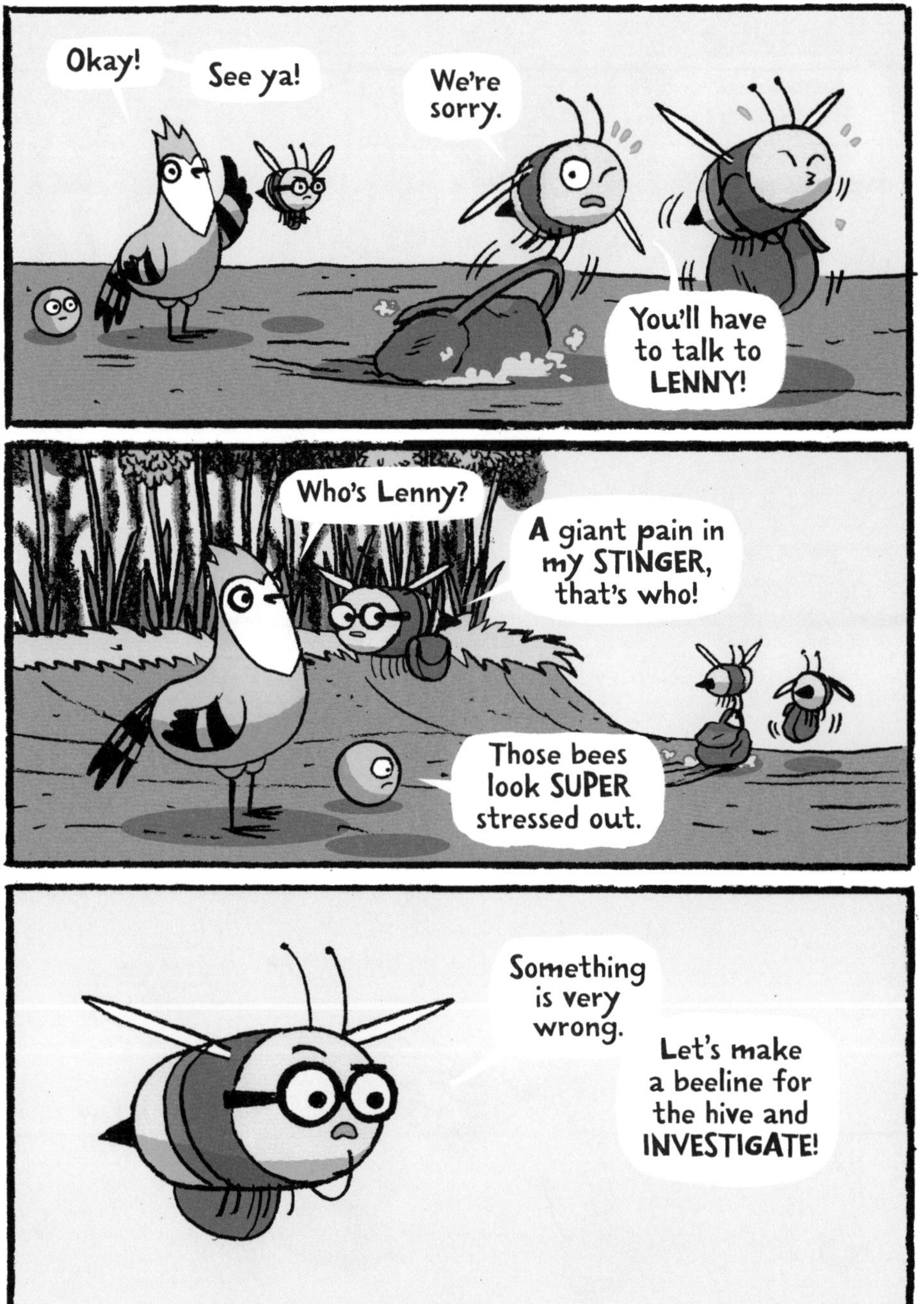

Okay!
See ya!
We're sorry.
You'll have to talk to LENNY!
Who's Lenny?
A giant pain in my STINGER, that's who!
Those bees look SUPER stressed out.
Something is very wrong.
Let's make a beeline for the hive and INVESTIGATE!

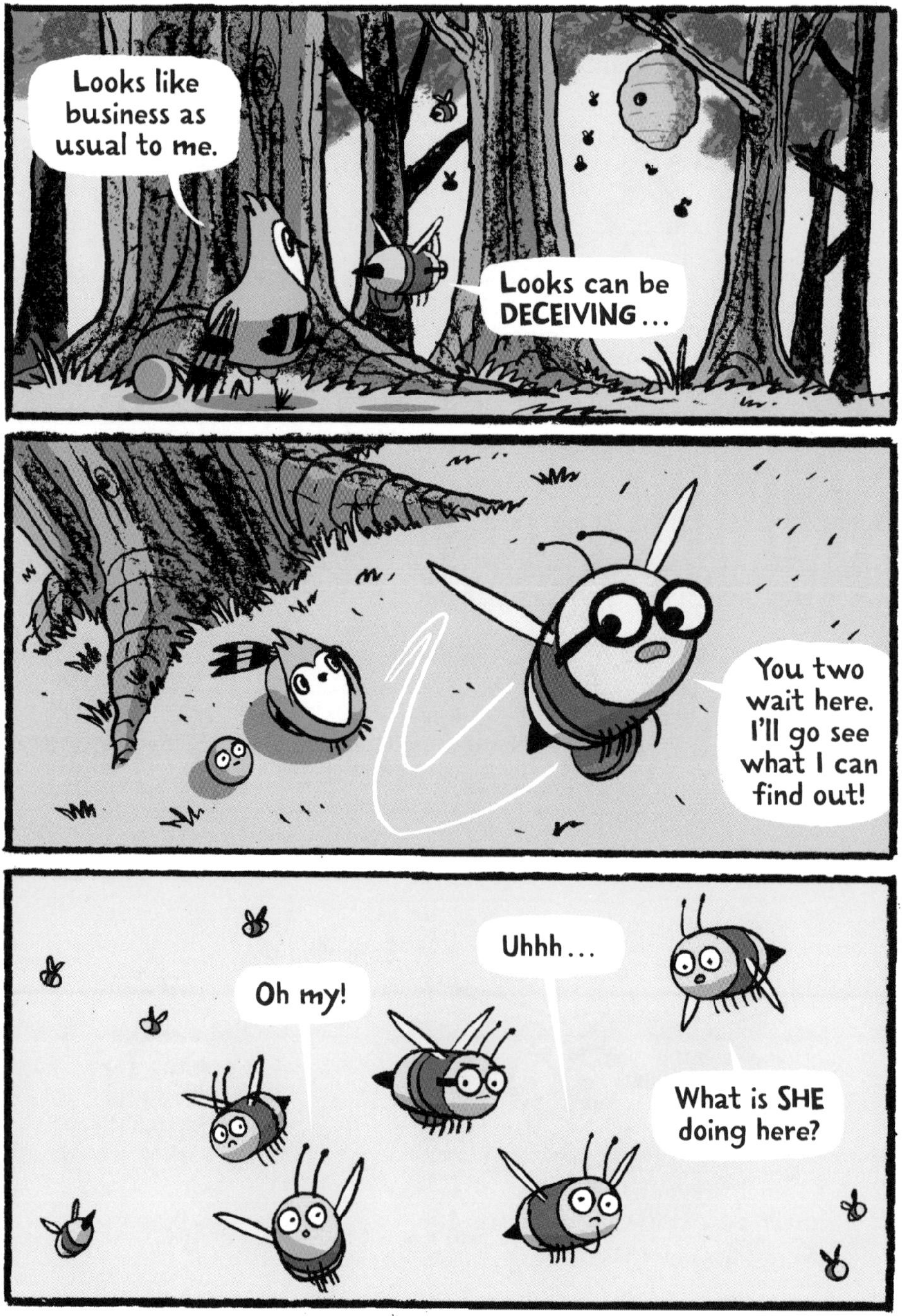
Looks like business as usual to me.
Looks can be DECEIVING...
You two wait here. I'll go see what I can find out!
Oh my!
Uhhh...
What is SHE doing here?

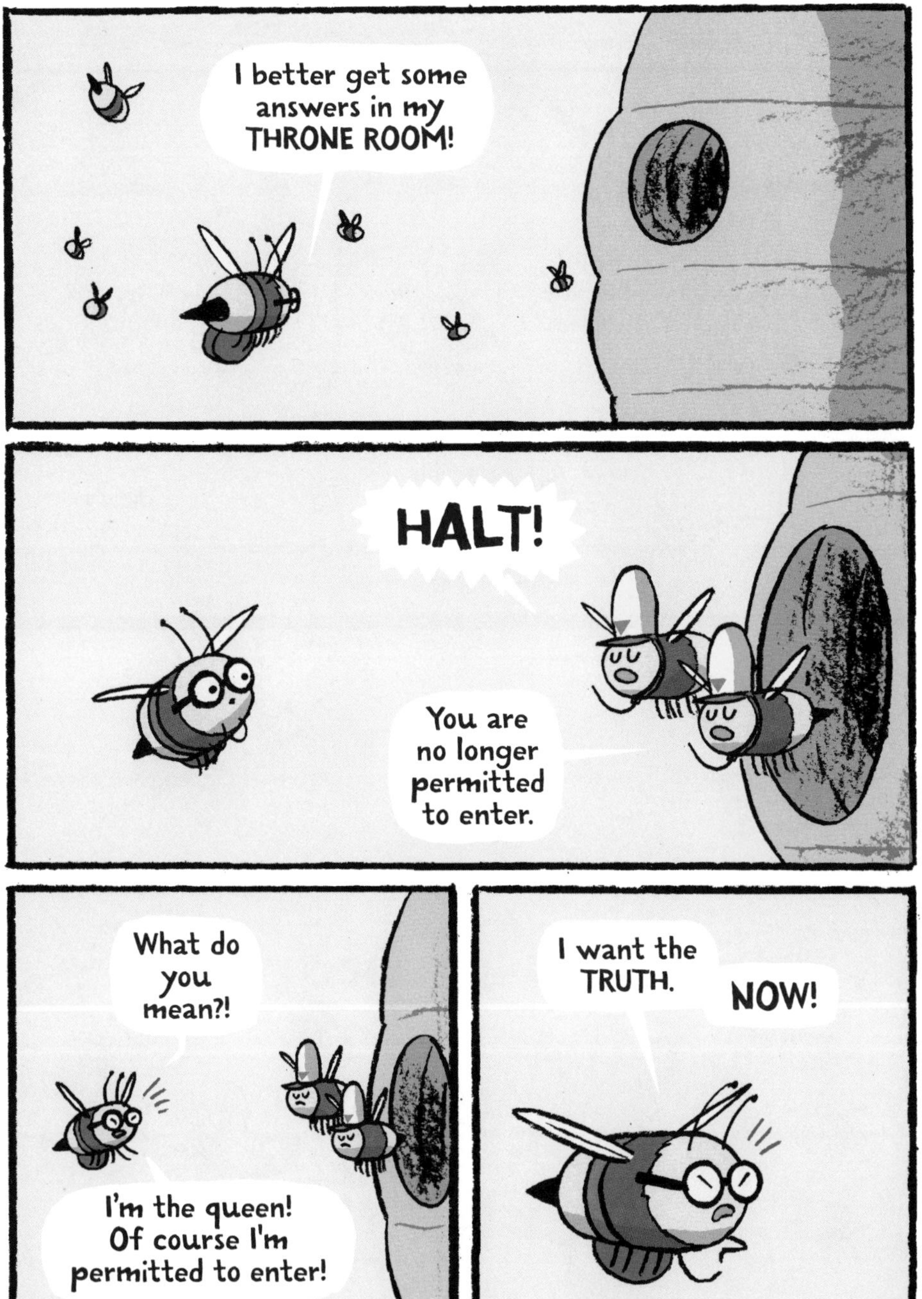

I better get some answers in my THRONE ROOM!
HALT!
You are no longer permitted to enter.
What do you mean?!
I'm the queen! Of course I'm permitted to enter!
I want the TRUTH.
NOW!

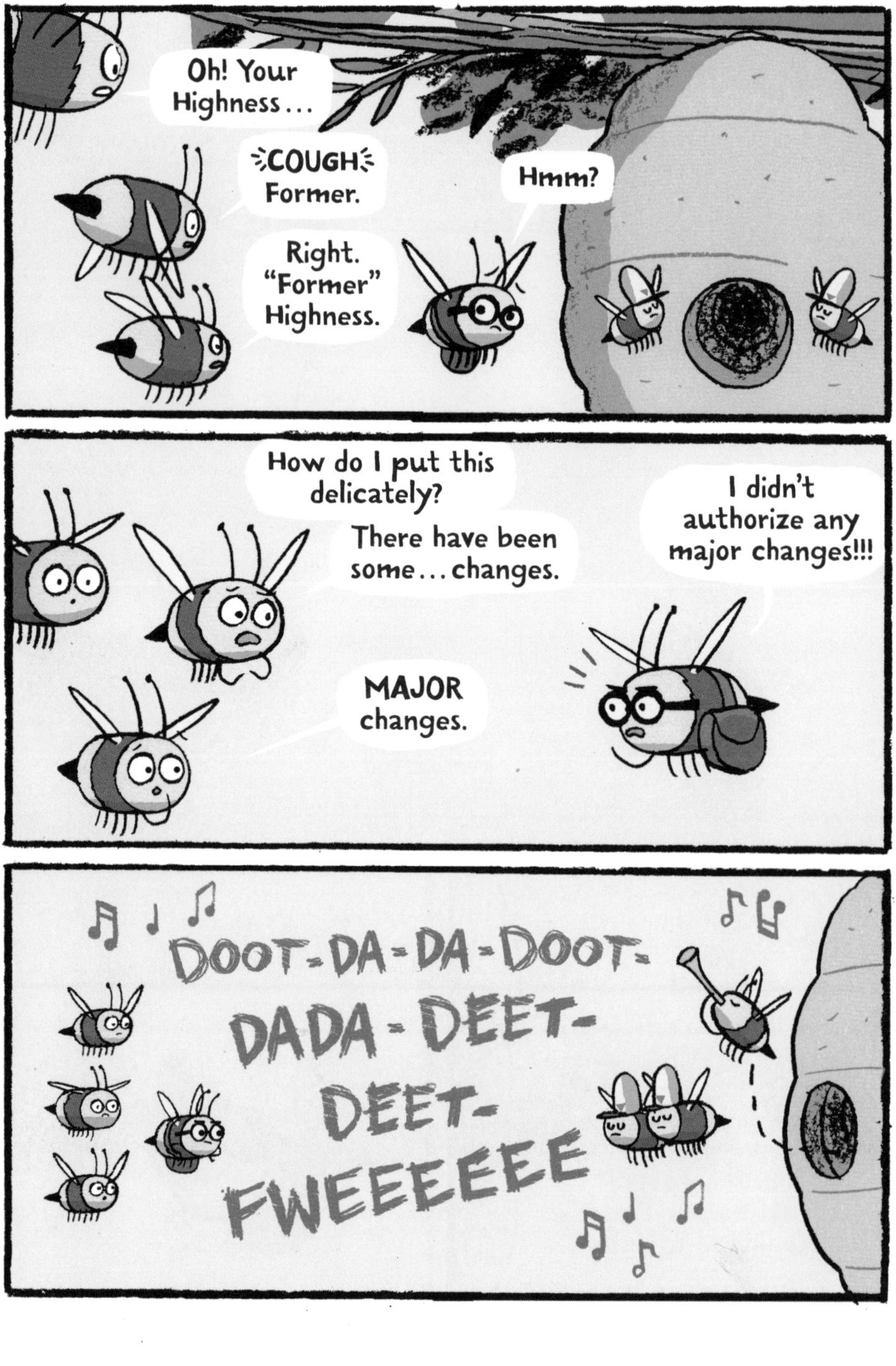

Oh! Your Highness...
COUGH Former.
Right. "Former" Highness.
Hmm?
How do I put this delicately?
There have been some... changes.
MAJOR changes.
I didn't authorize any major changes!!!
DOOT-DA-DA-DOOT-
DADA-DEET-
DEET-
FWEEEEEE

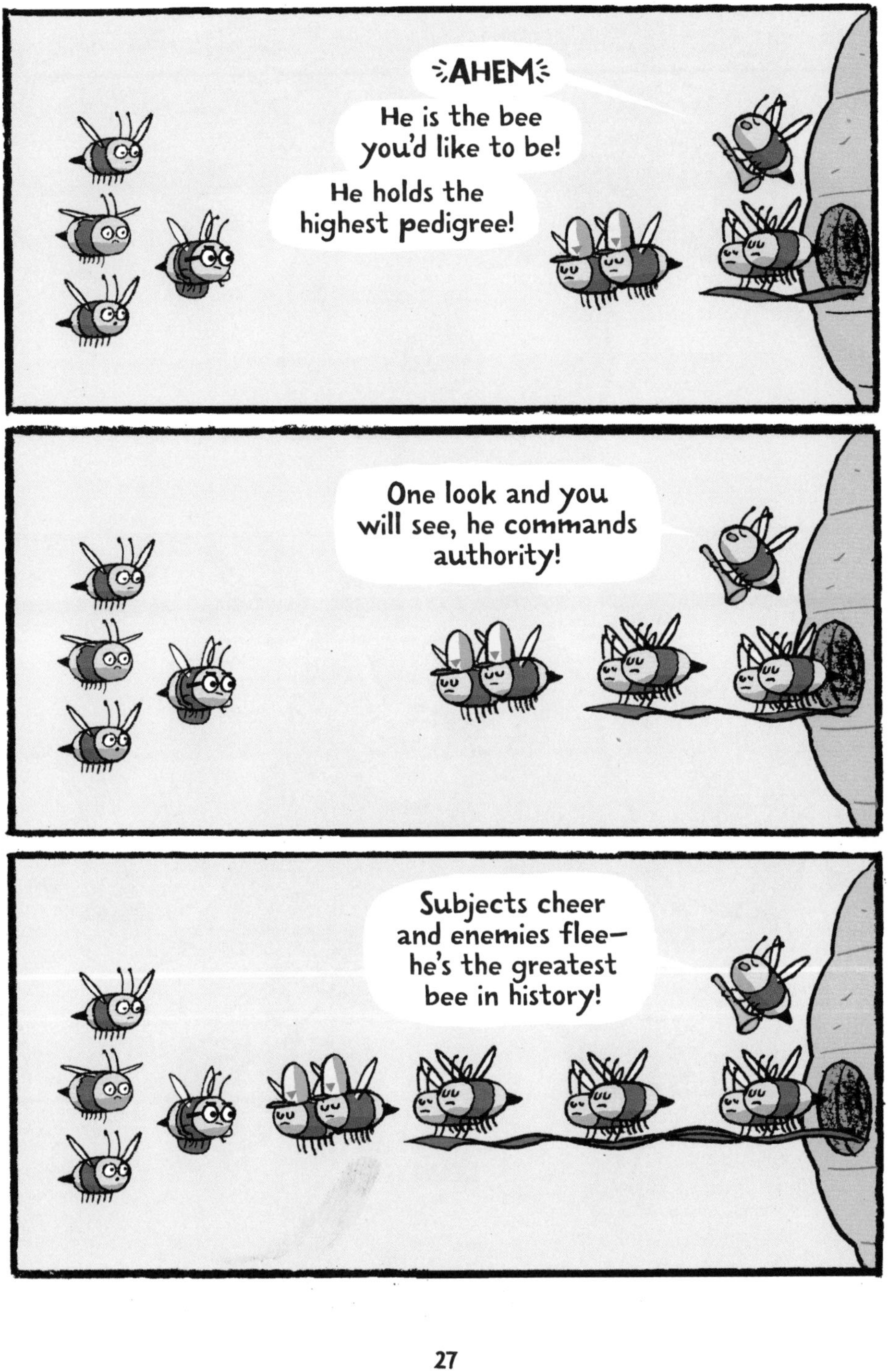
AHEM
He is the bee you'd like to be!
He holds the highest pedigree!
One look and you will see, he commands authority!
Subjects cheer and enemies flee—he's the greatest bee in history!

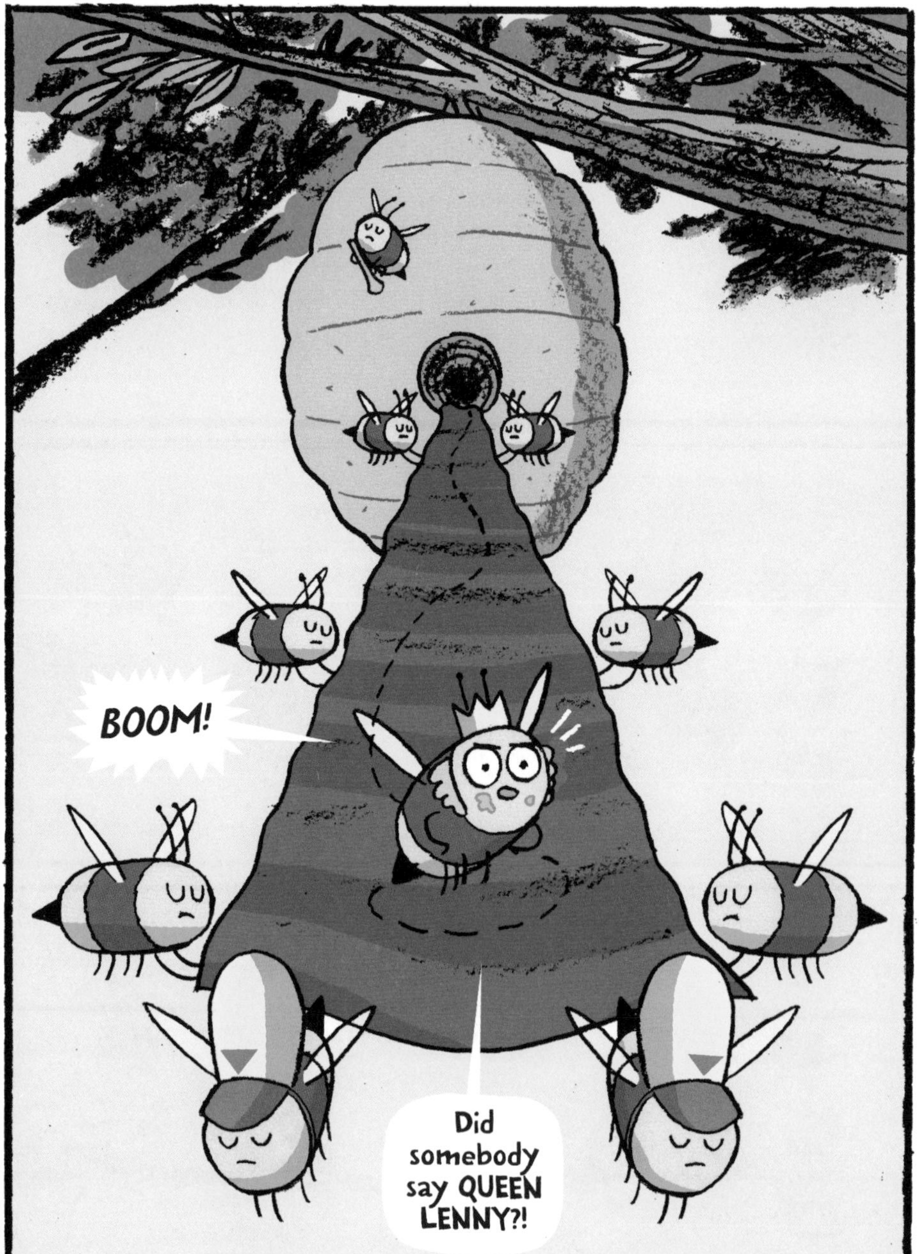
BOOM!
Did somebody say QUEEN LENNY?!

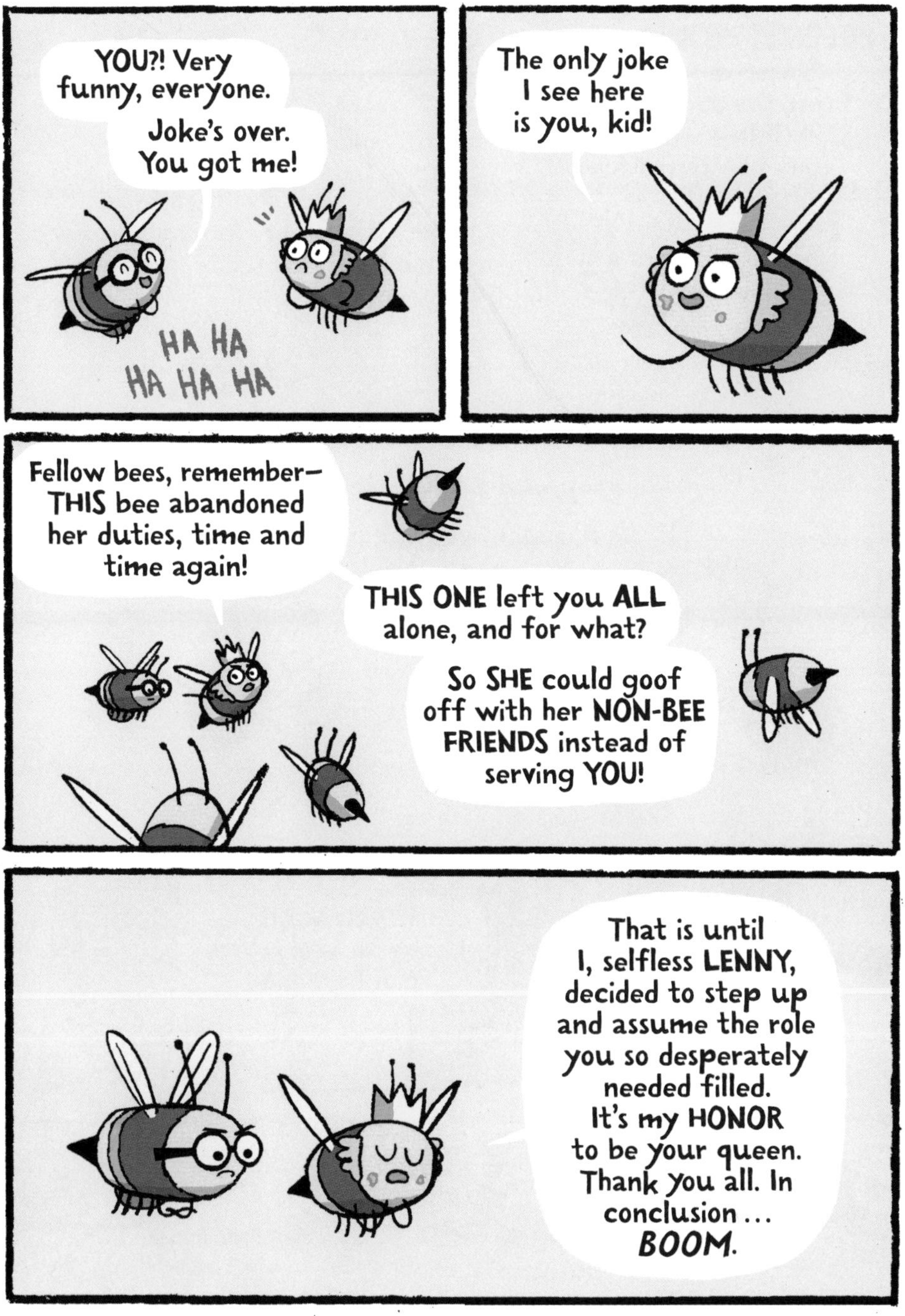
YOU?! Very funny, everyone.
Joke's over. You got me!
HA HA HA HA HA
The only joke I see here is you, kid!
Fellow bees, remember— THIS bee abandoned her duties, time and time again!
THIS ONE left you ALL alone, and for what?
So SHE could goof off with her NON-BEE FRIENDS instead of serving YOU!
That is until I, selfless LENNY, decided to step up and assume the role you so desperately needed filled. It's my HONOR to be your queen. Thank you all. In conclusion ... BOOM.

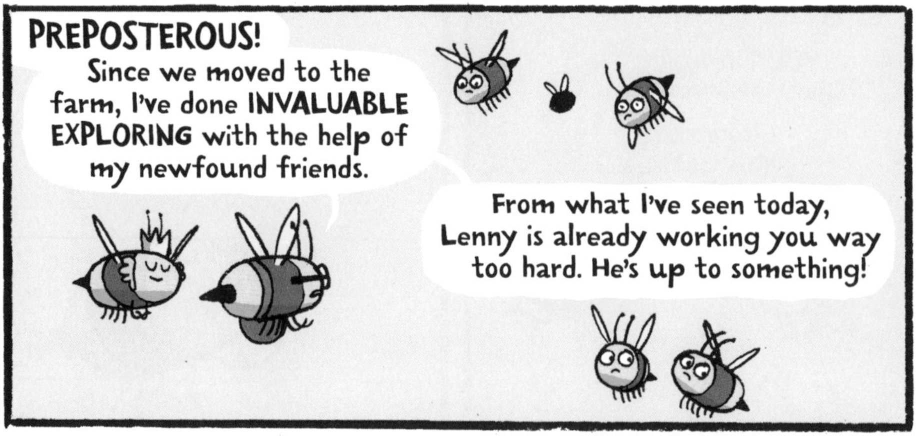
PREPOSTEROUS! Since we moved to the farm, I've done INVALUABLE EXPLORING with the help of my newfound friends.
From what I've seen today, Lenny is already working you way too hard. He's up to something!

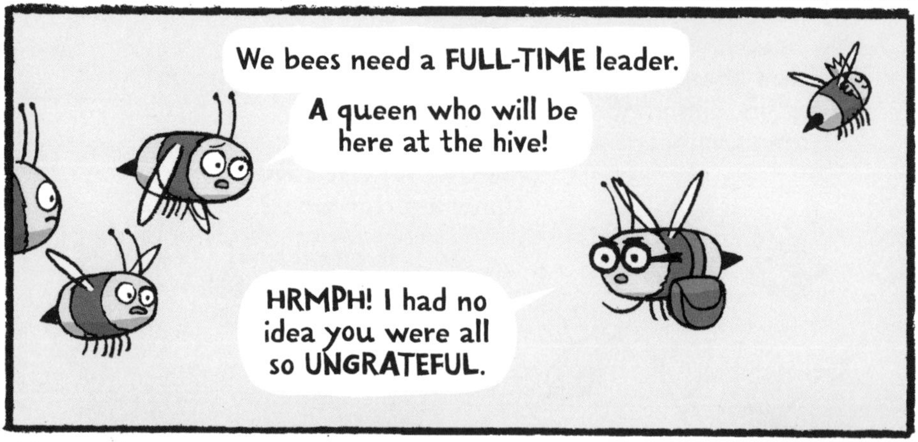
We bees need a FULL-TIME leader.
A queen who will be here at the hive!
HRMPH! I had no idea you were all so UNGRATEFUL.

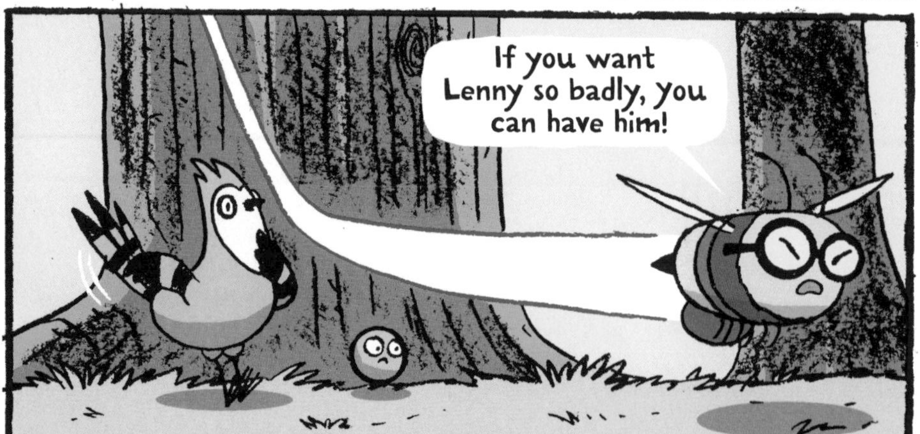
If you want Lenny so badly, you can have him!

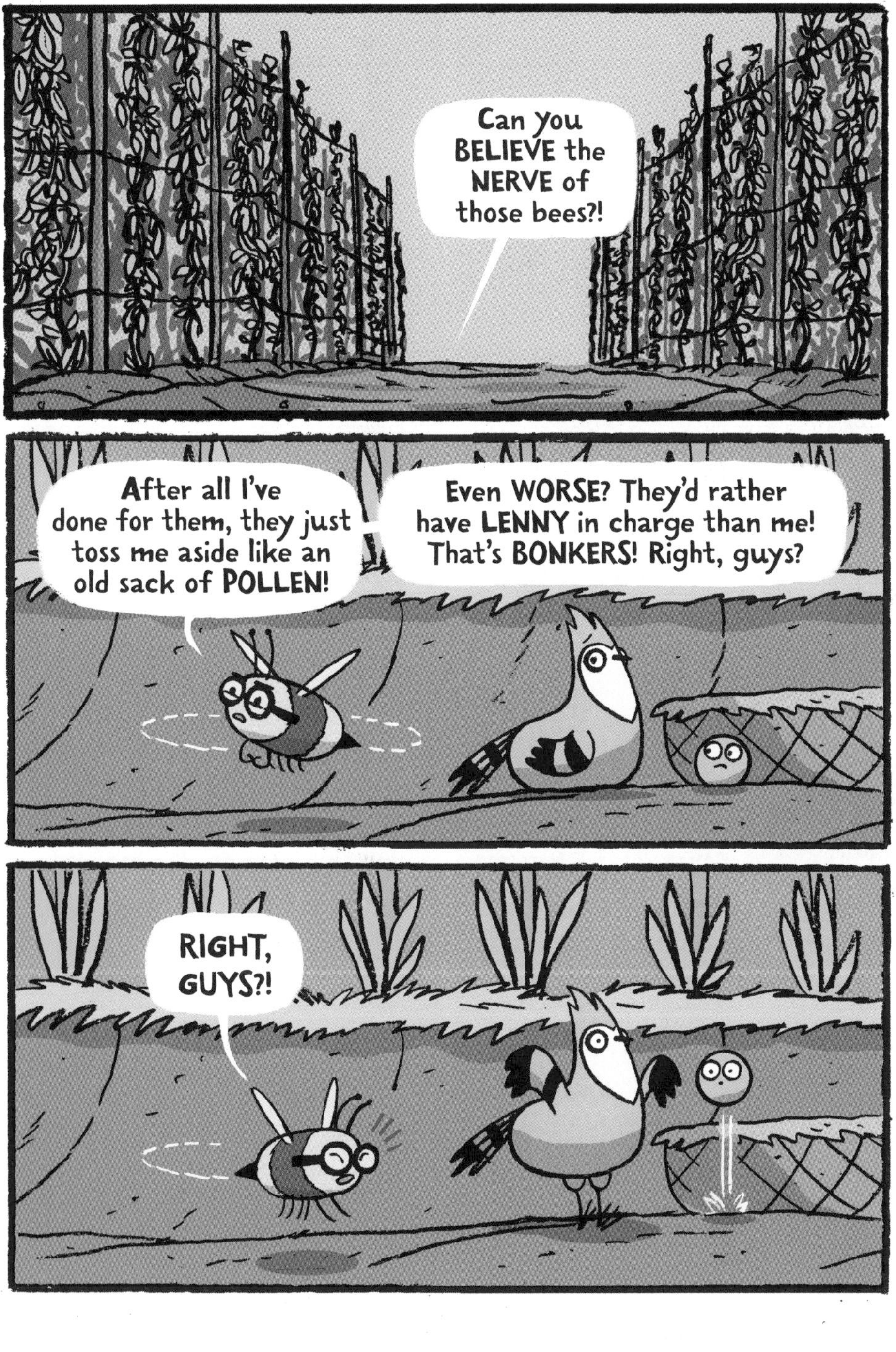
Can you BELIEVE the NERVE of those bees?!
After all I've done for them, they just toss me aside like an old sack of POLLEN!
Even WORSE? They'd rather have LENNY in charge than me! That's BONKERS! Right, guys?
RIGHT, GUYS?!

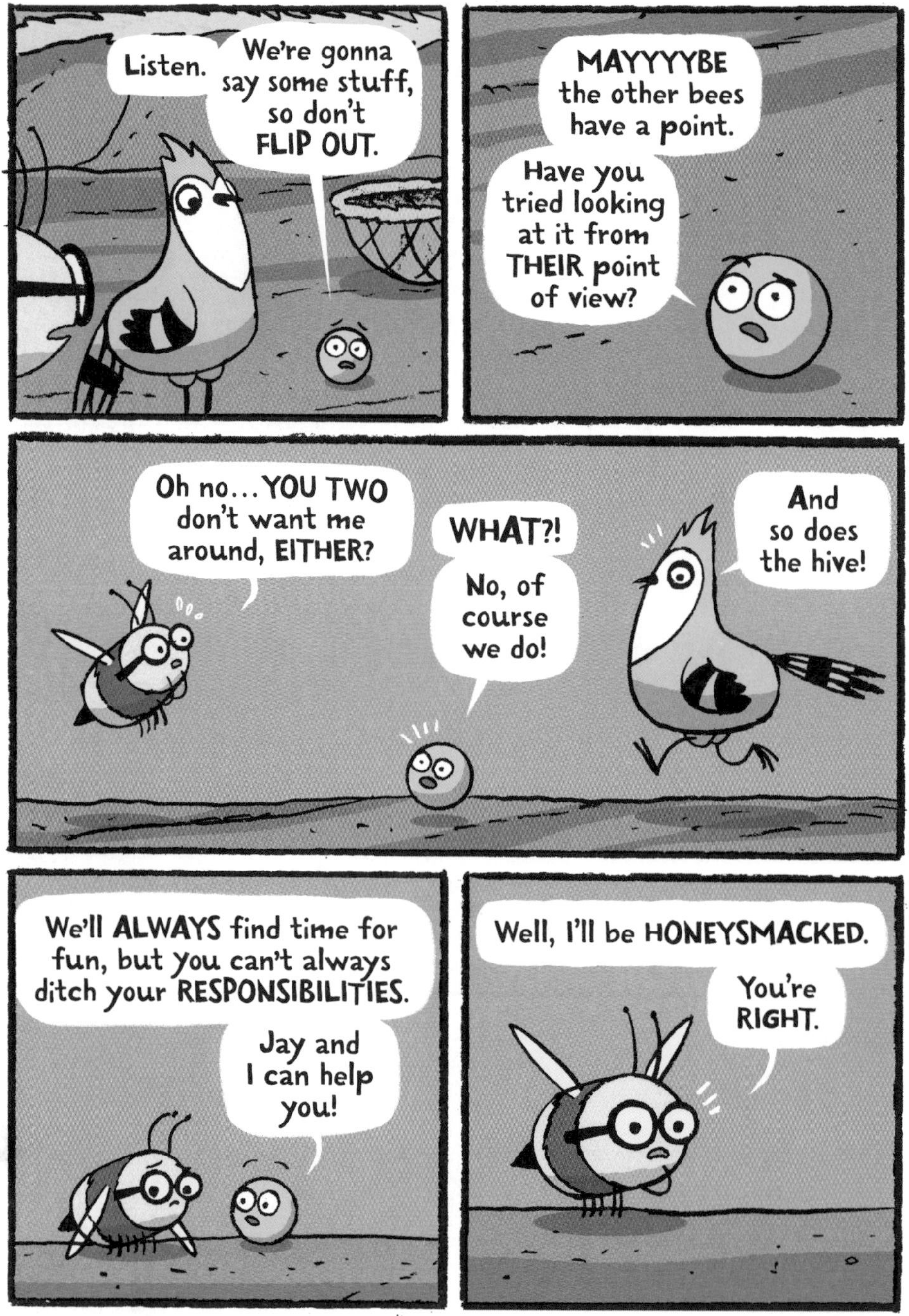
Listen.
We're gonna say some stuff, so don't FLIP OUT.
MAYYYYBE the other bees have a point.
Have you tried looking at it from THEIR point of view?
Oh no... YOU TWO don't want me around, EITHER?
WHAT?!
No, of course we do!
And so does the hive!
We'll ALWAYS find time for fun, but you can't always ditch your RESPONSIBILITIES.
Jay and I can help you!
Well, I'll be HONEYSMACKED.
You're RIGHT.

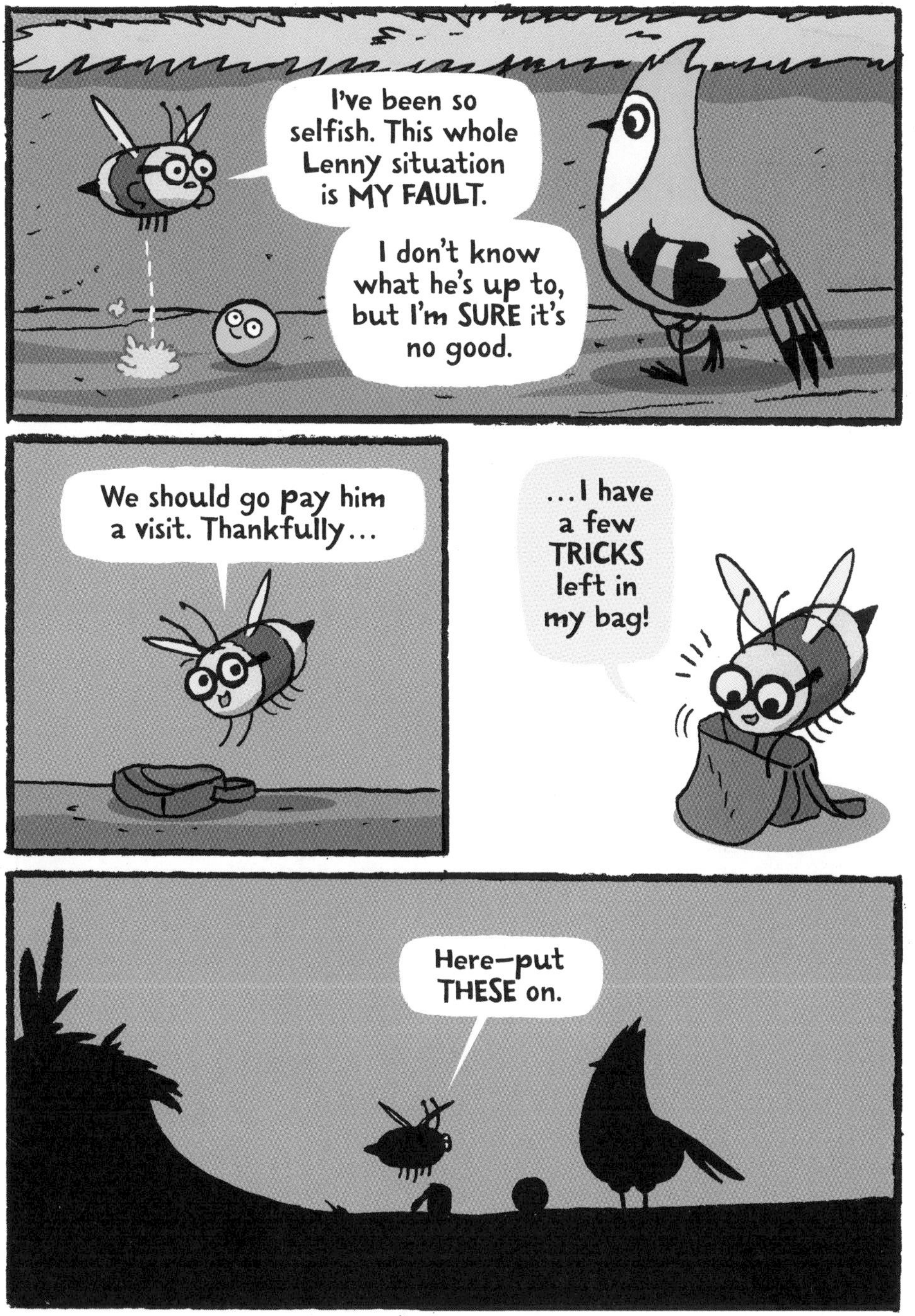
I've been so selfish. This whole Lenny situation is MY FAULT.
I don't know what he's up to, but I'm SURE it's no good.
We should go pay him a visit. Thankfully...
...I have a few TRICKS left in my bag!
Here—put THESE on.

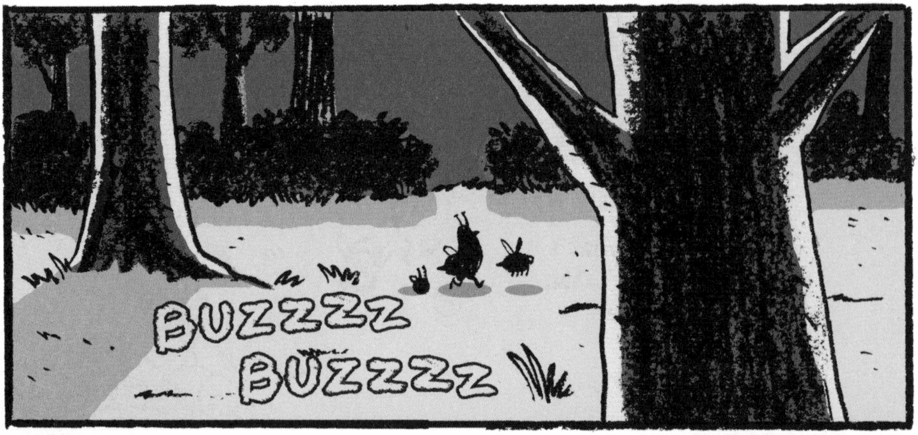
BUZZZZ
BUZZZZ

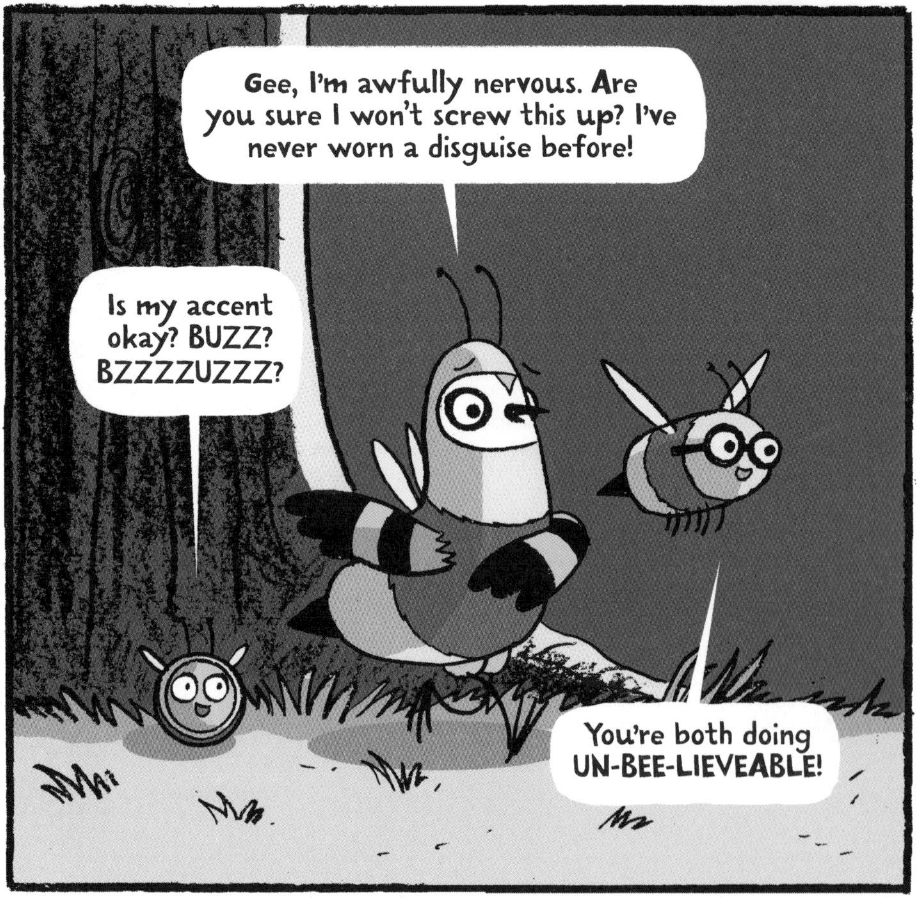
Gee, I'm awfully nervous. Are you sure I won't screw this up? I've never worn a disguise before!
Is my accent okay? BUZZ? BZZZZUZZZ?
You're both doing UN-BEE-LIEVEABLE!

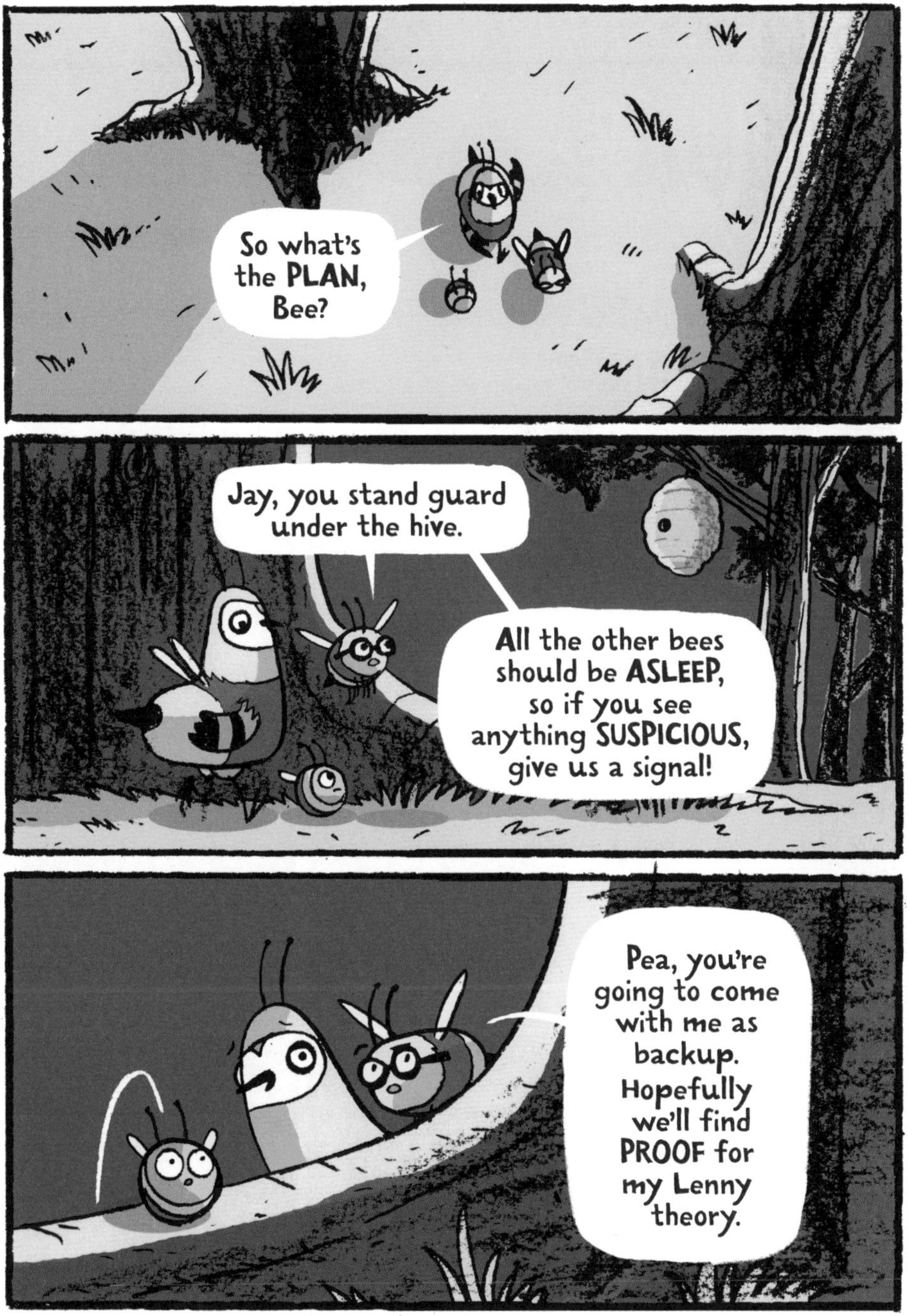
So what's the PLAN, Bee?
Jay, you stand guard under the hive.
All the other bees should be ASLEEP, so if you see anything SUSPICIOUS, give us a signal!
Pea, you're going to come with me as backup. Hopefully we'll find PROOF for my Lenny theory.

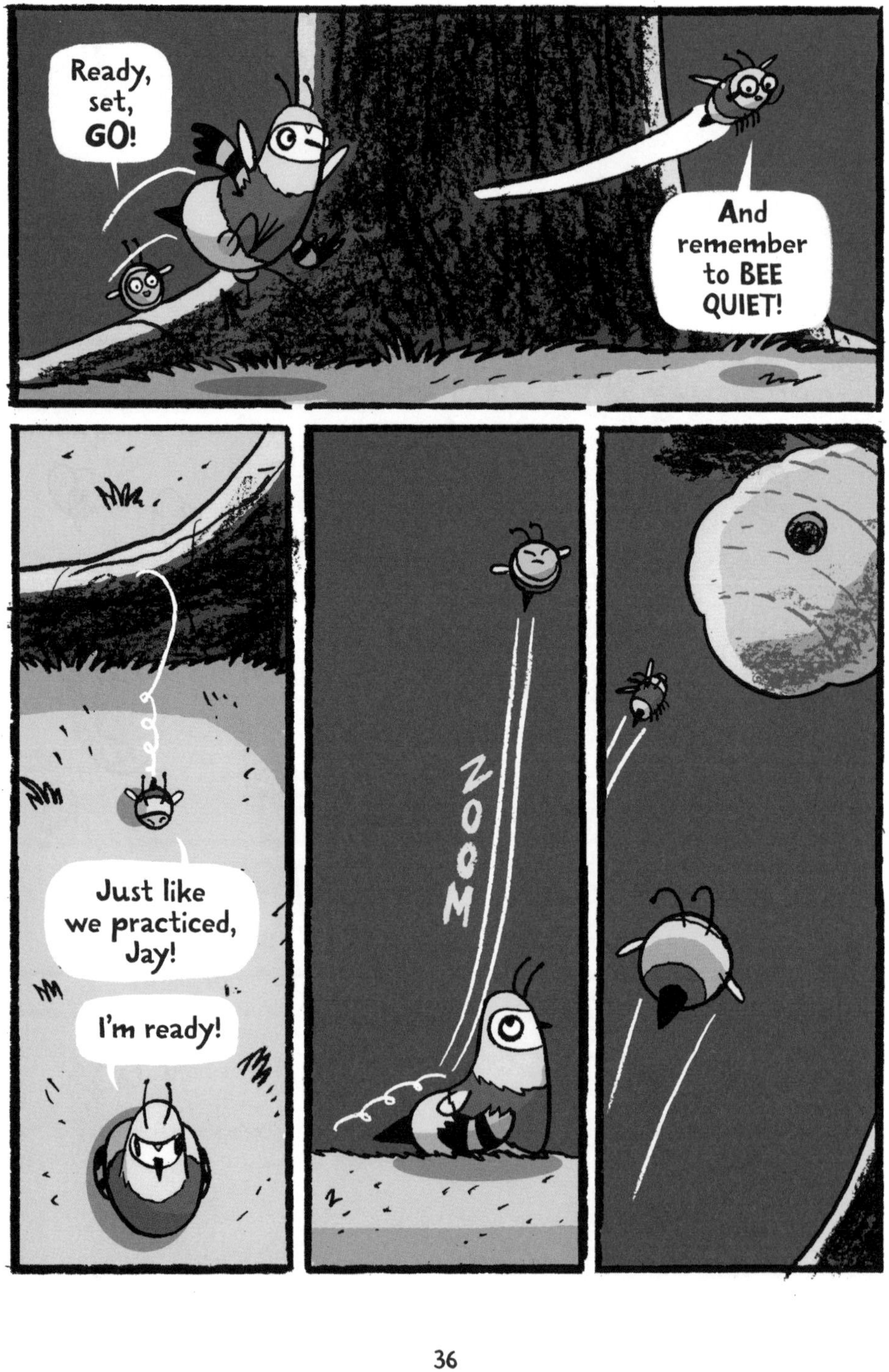
Ready, set, GO!
And remember to BEE QUIET!
Just like we practiced, Jay!
I'm ready!
ZOOM

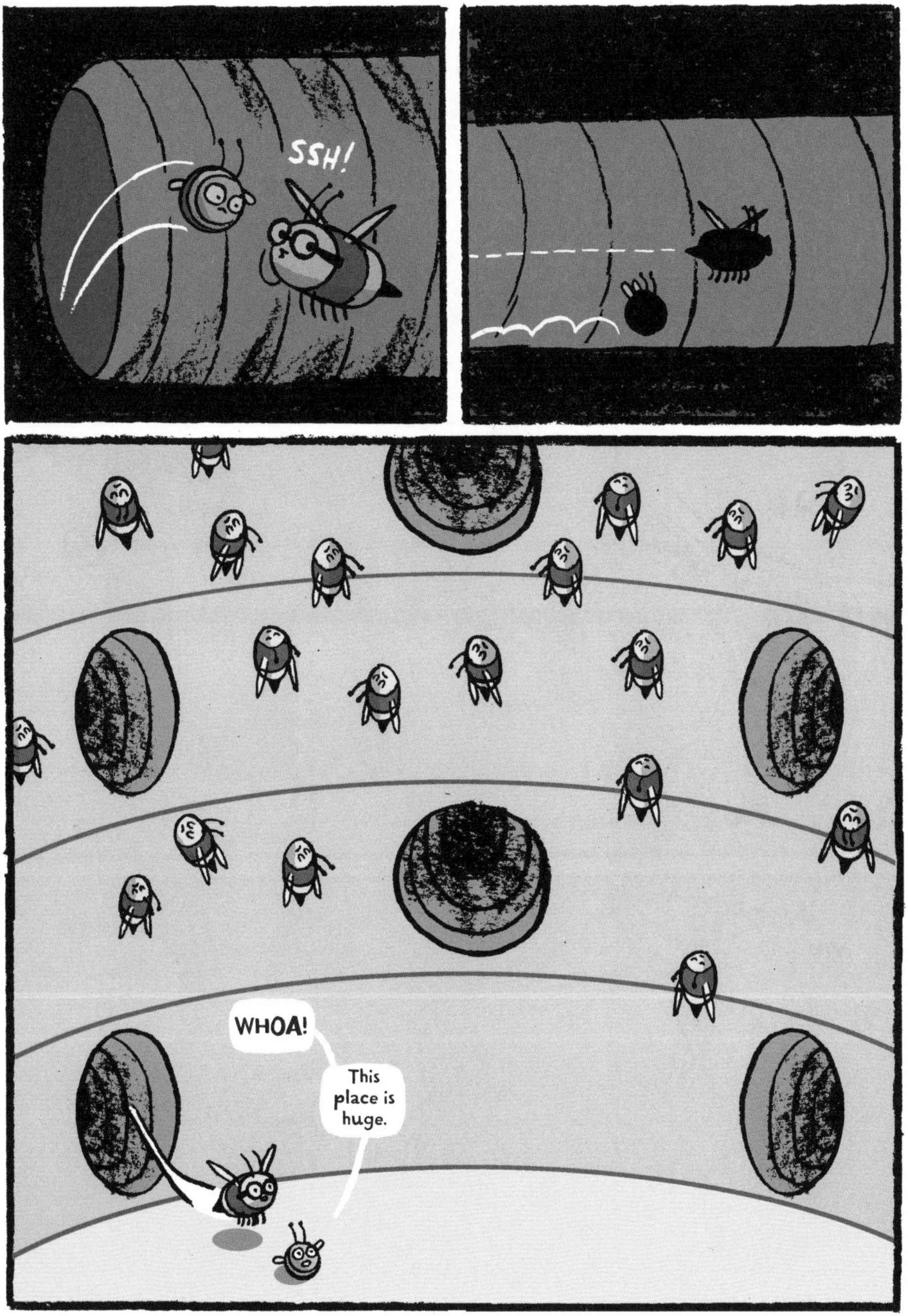
SSH!
WHOA!
This place is huge.

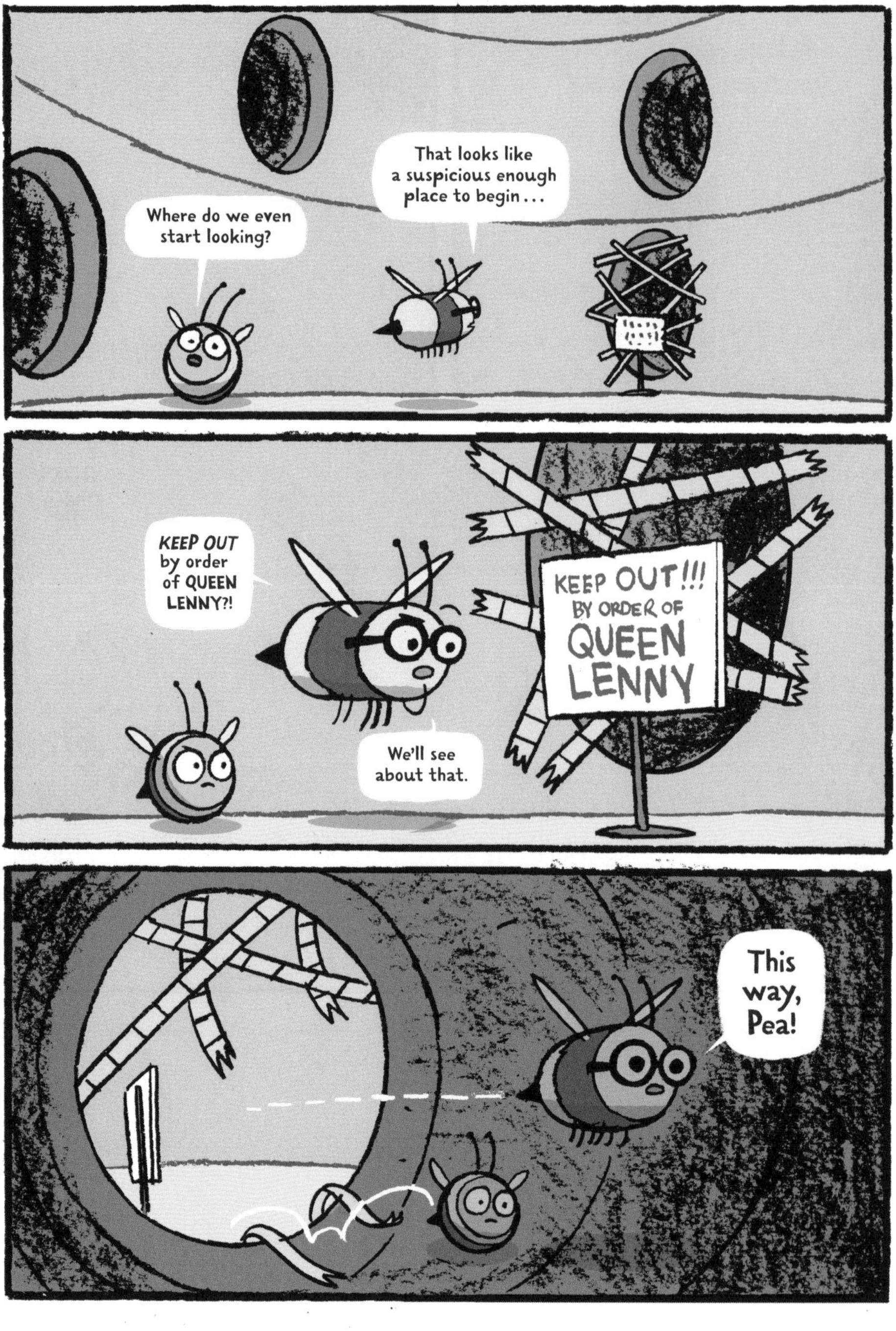
Where do we even start looking?
That looks like a suspicious enough place to begin...
KEEP OUT by order of QUEEN LENNY?!
KEEP OUT!!! BY ORDER OF QUEEN LENNY
We'll see about that.
This way, Pea!

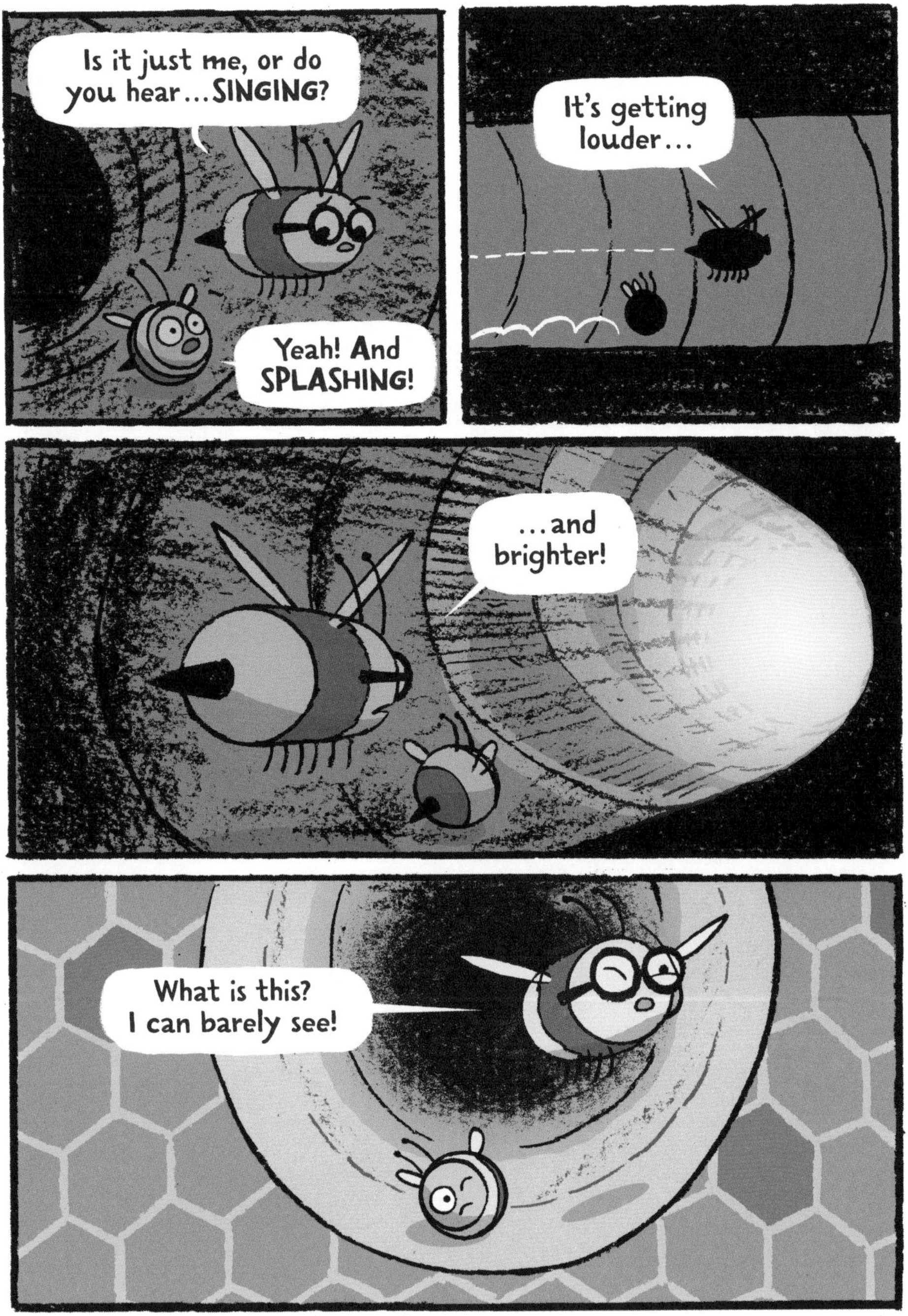
Is it just me, or do you hear...SINGING?
Yeah! And SPLASHING!
It's getting louder...
...and brighter!
What is this? I can barely see!

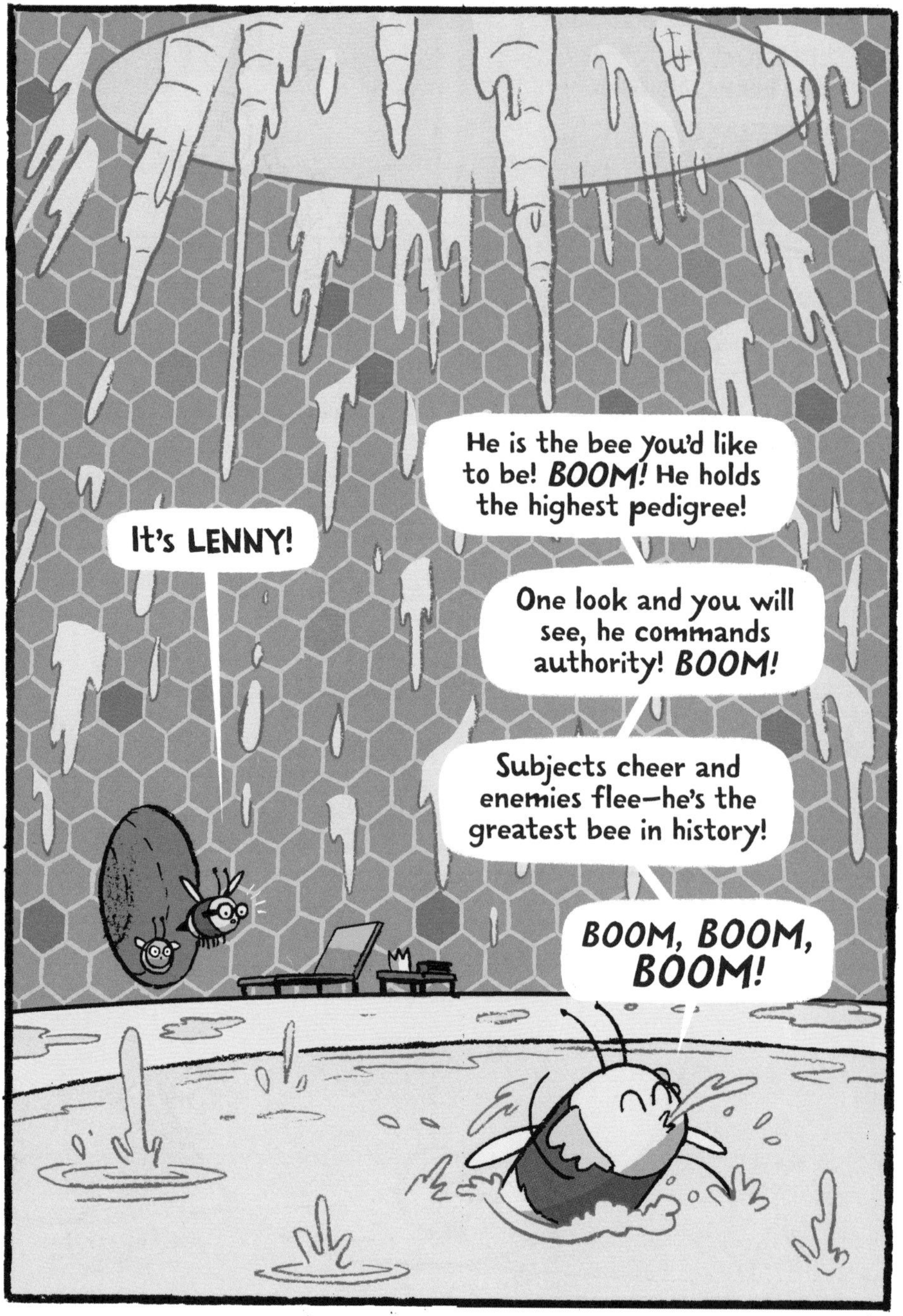

It's LENNY!
He is the bee you'd like to be! BOOM! He holds the highest pedigree!
One look and you will see, he commands authority! BOOM!
Subjects cheer and enemies flee—he's the greatest bee in history!
BOOM, BOOM, BOOM!

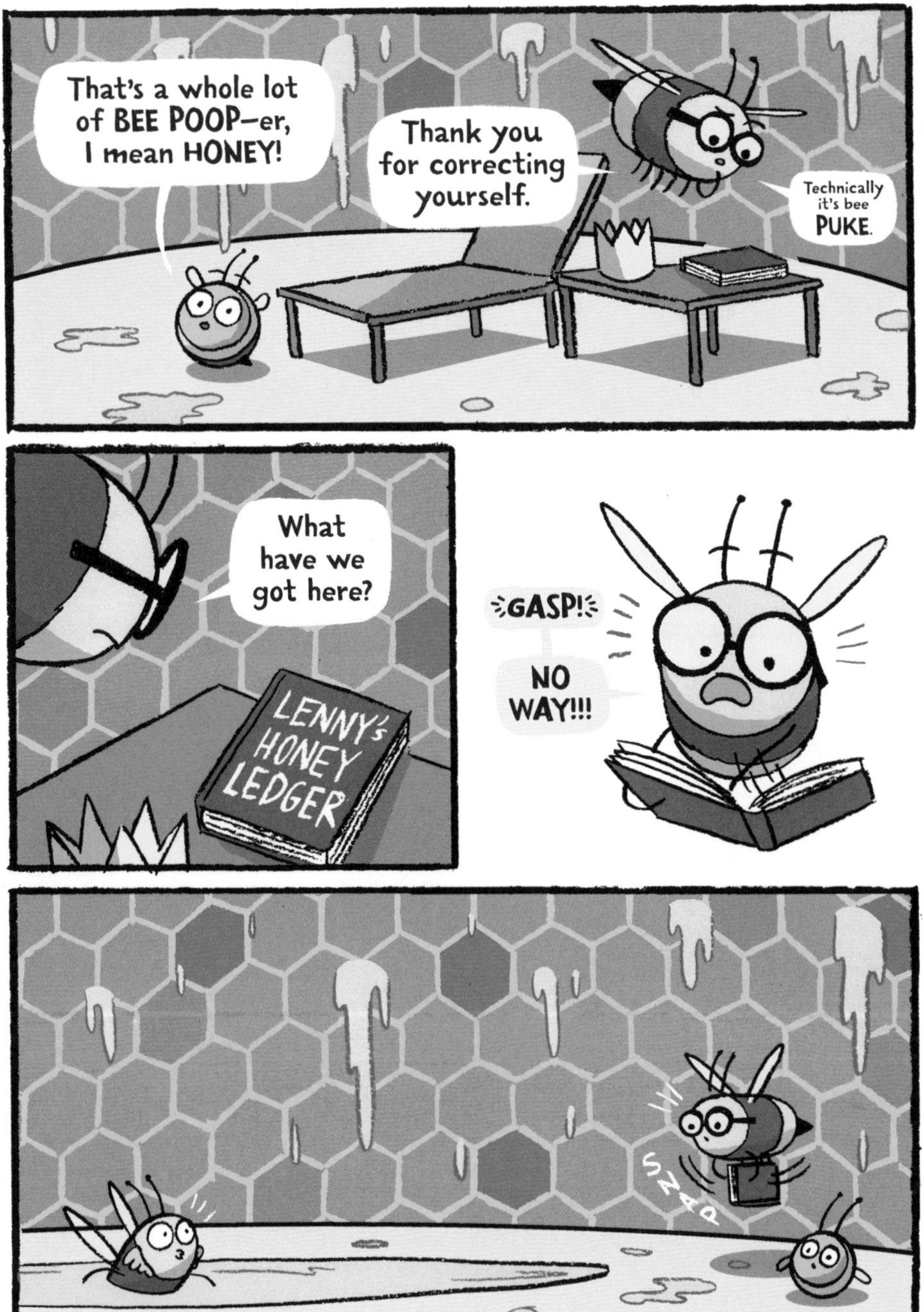

That's a whole lot of BEE POOP—er, I mean HONEY!
Thank you for correcting yourself.
Technically it's bee PUKE.
What have we got here?
LENNY's HONEY LEDGER
GASP!
NO WAY!!!
SNAP

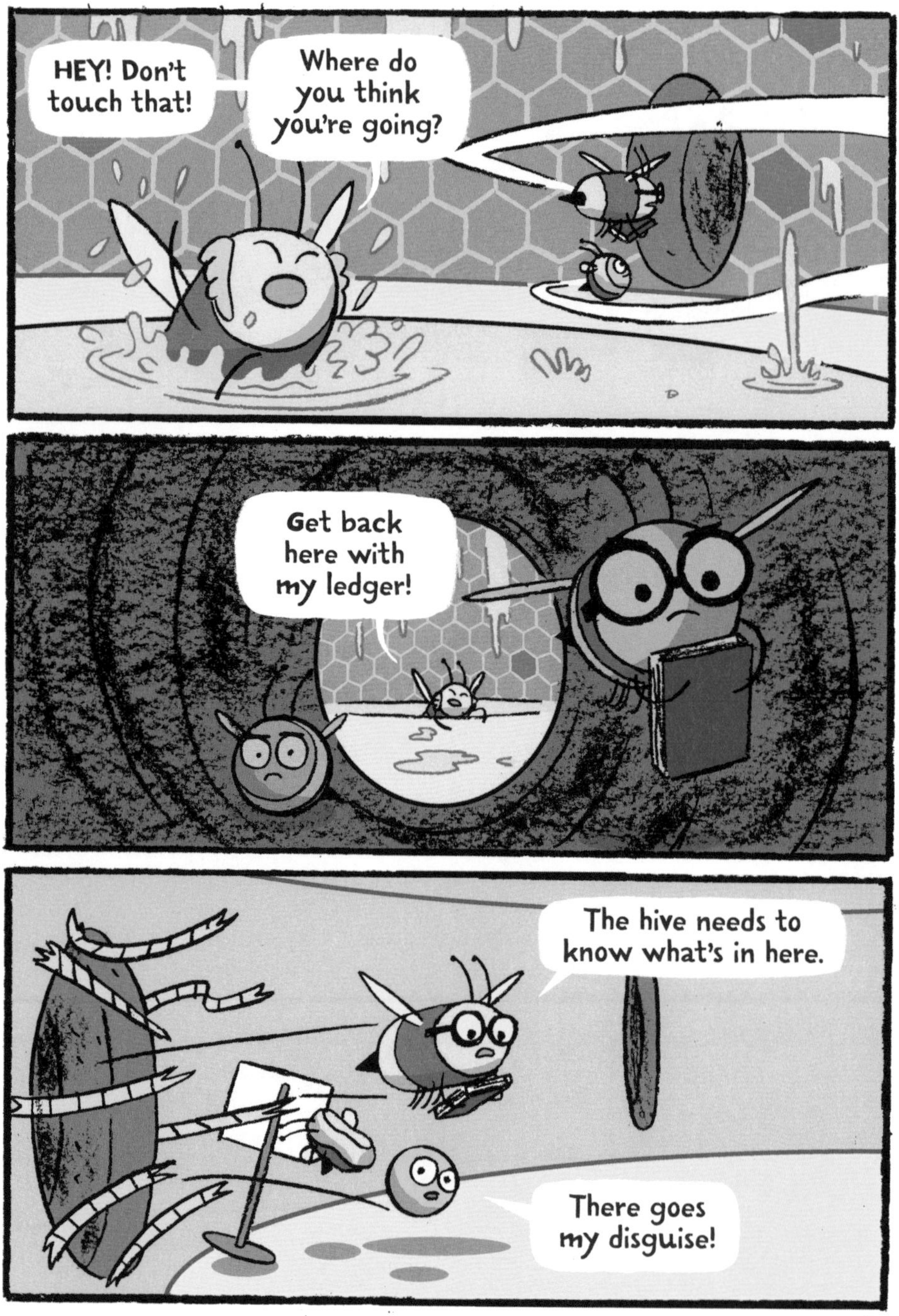
HEY! Don't touch that!
Where do you think you're going?
Get back here with my ledger!
The hive needs to know what's in here.
There goes my disguise!

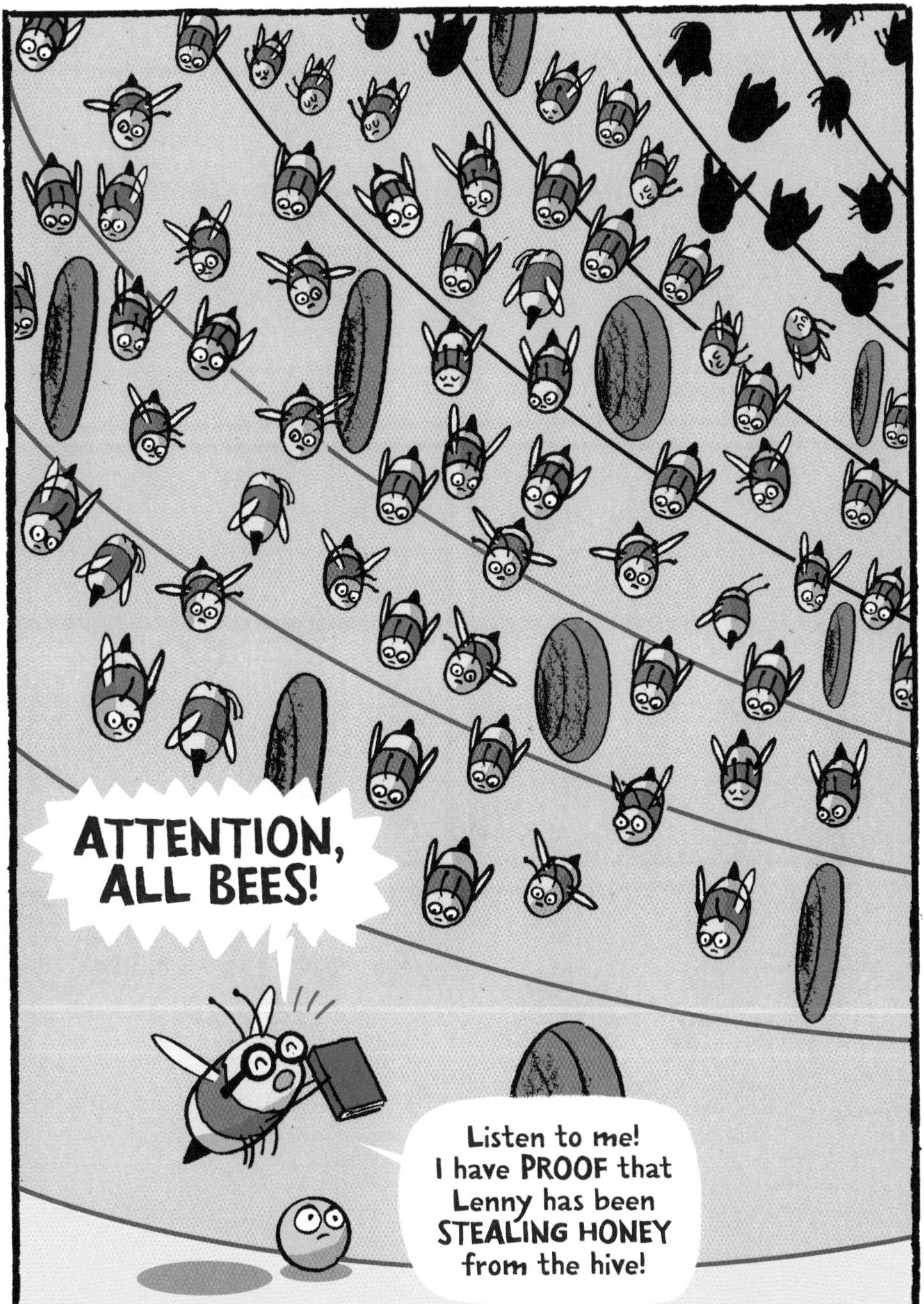
ATTENTION, ALL BEES!
Listen to me! I have PROOF that Lenny has been STEALING HONEY from the hive!

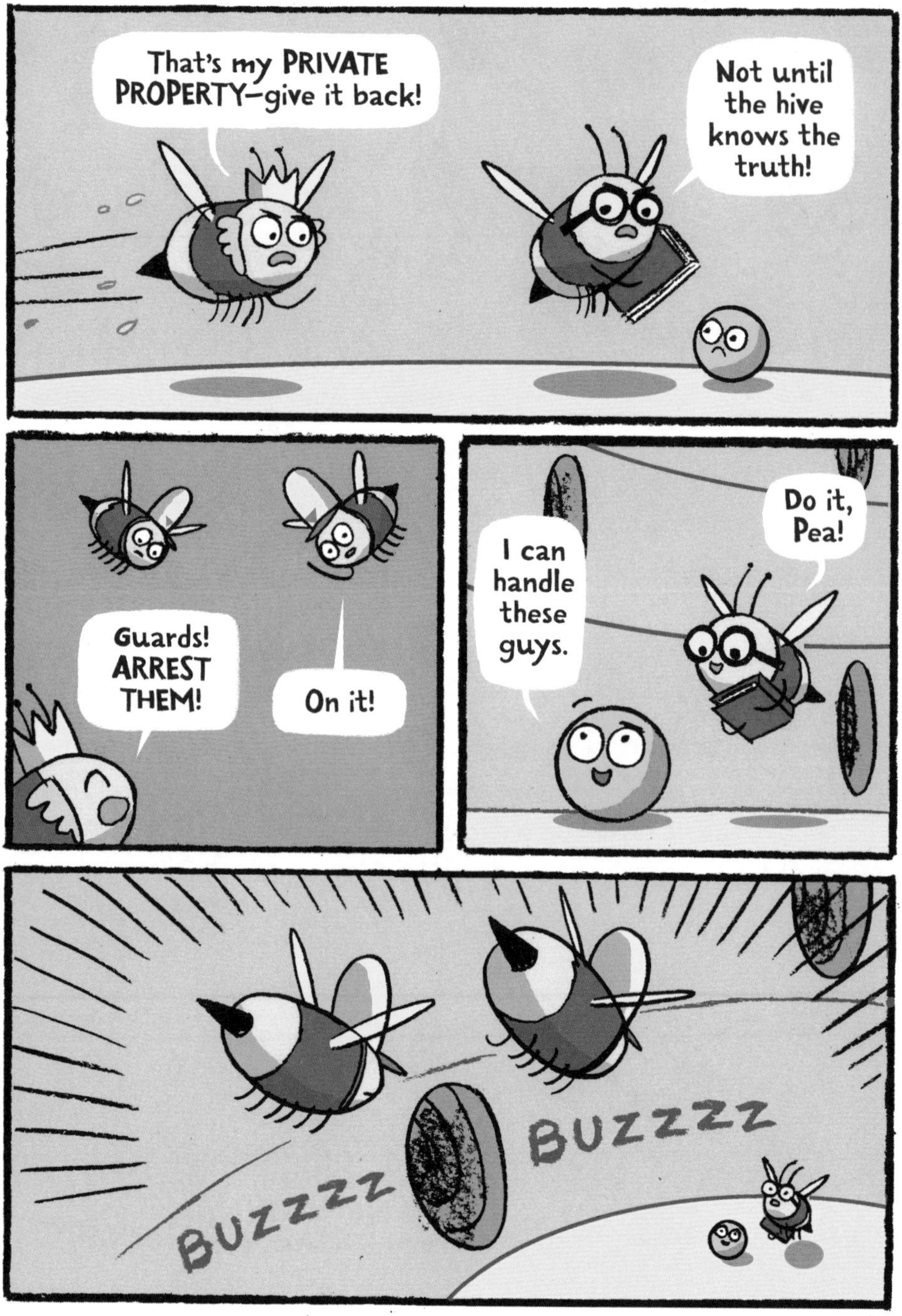
That's my PRIVATE PROPERTY—give it back!
Not until the hive knows the truth!
Guards! ARREST THEM!
On it!
I can handle these guys.
Do it, Pea!
BUZZZZ
BUZZZZ

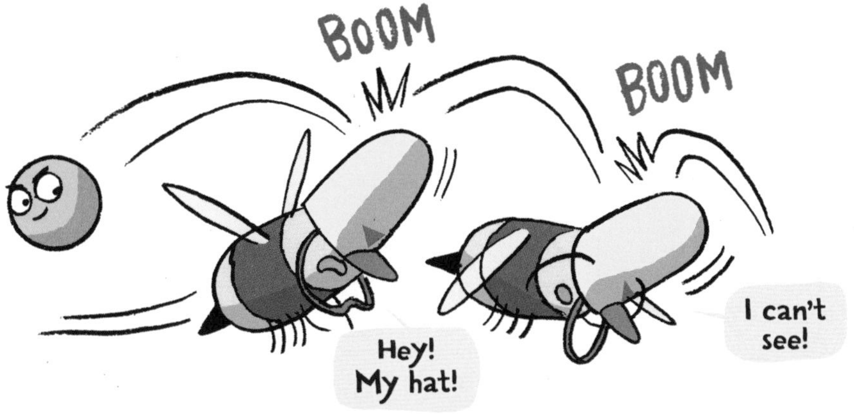
BOOM
BOOM
Hey! My hat!
I can't see!

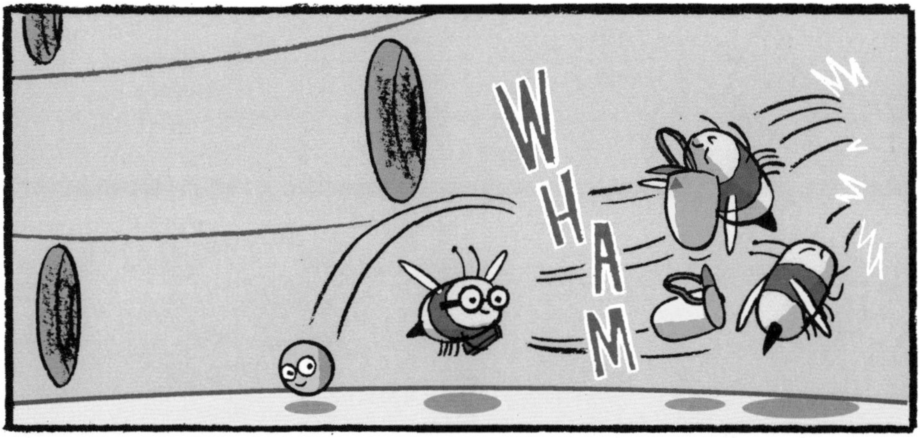
WHAM

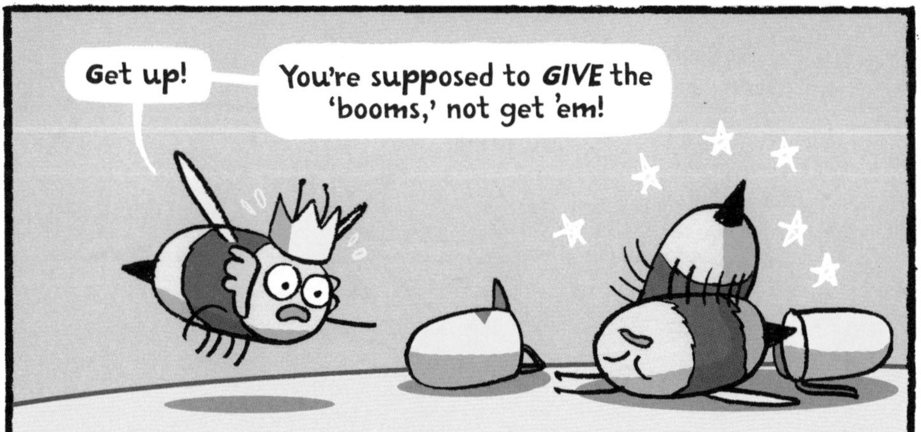
Get up!
You're supposed to *GIVE* the 'booms,' not get 'em!

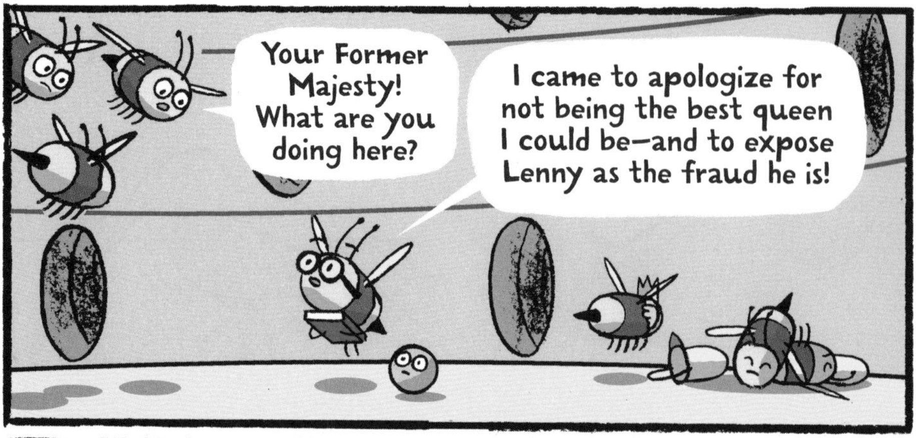
Your Former Majesty! What are you doing here?
I came to apologize for not being the best queen I could be—and to expose Lenny as the fraud he is!

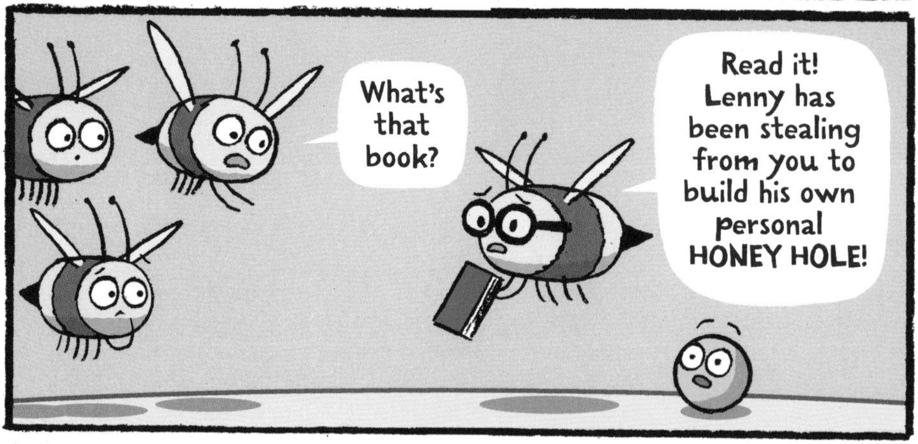
What's that book?
Read it! Lenny has been stealing from you to build his own personal HONEY HOLE!

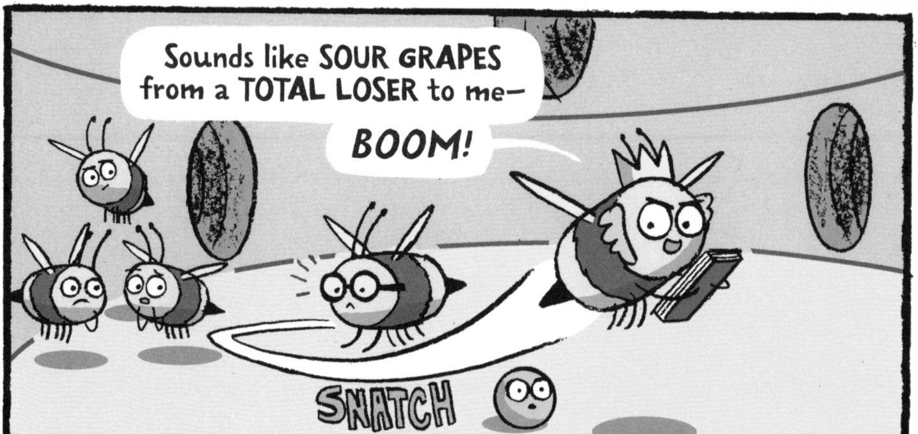
Sounds like SOUR GRAPES from a TOTAL LOSER to me—
BOOM!
SNATCH

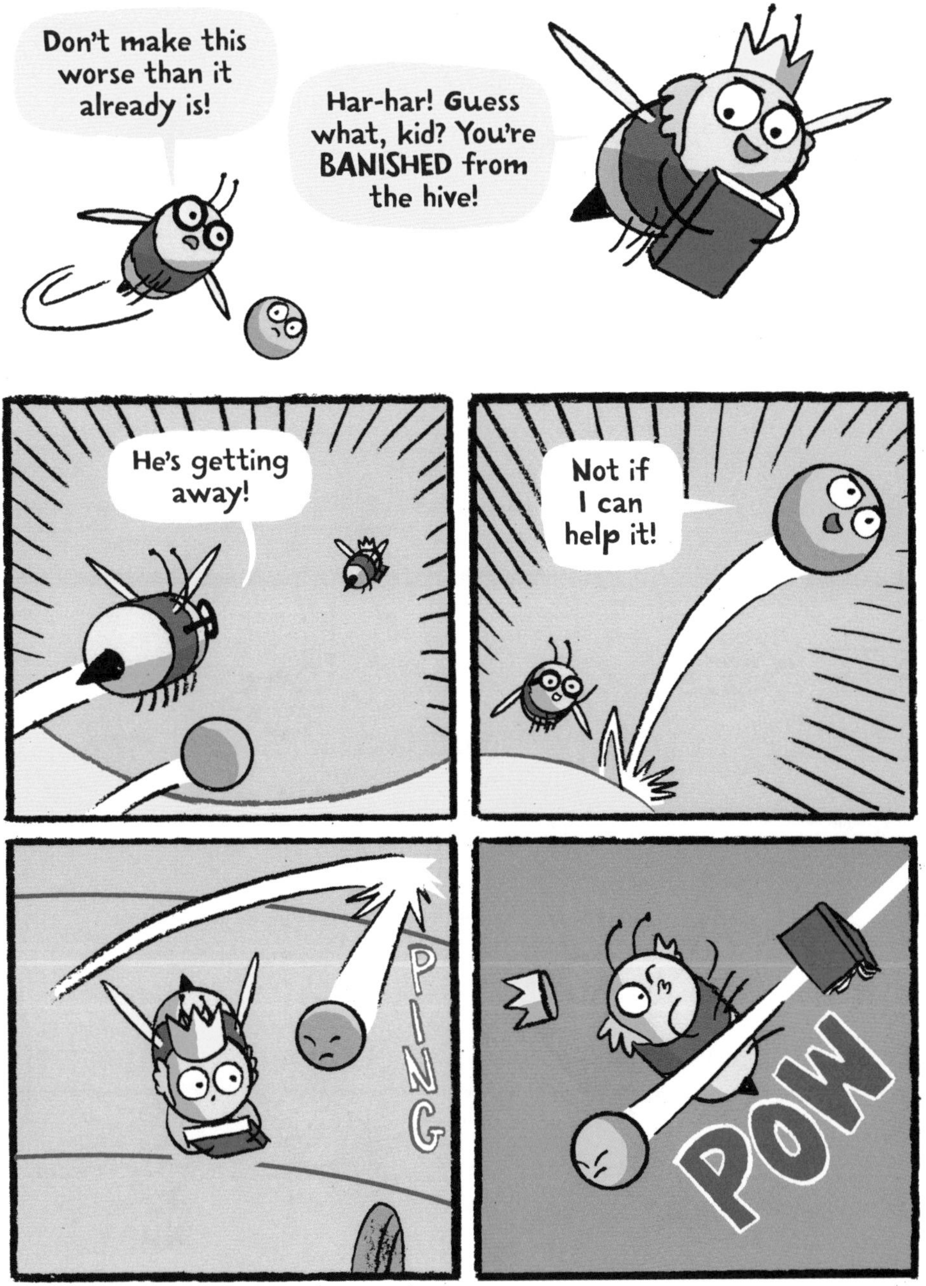
Don't make this worse than it already is!
Har-har! Guess what, kid? You're BANISHED from the hive!
He's getting away!
Not if I can help it!
PING
POW

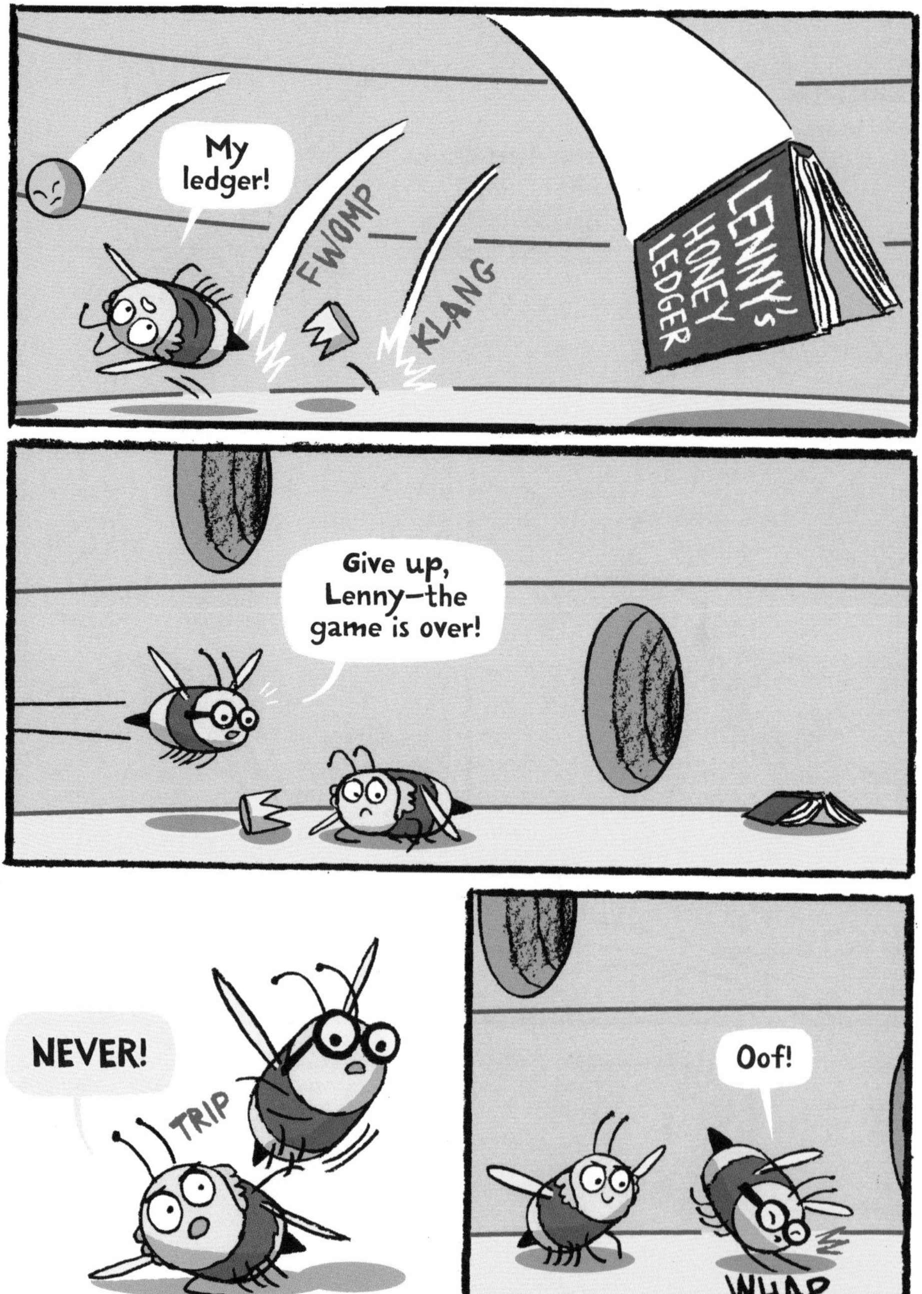
My ledger!
FWOMP
KLANG
LENNY'S HONEY LEDGER
Give up, Lenny—the game is over!
NEVER!
TRIP
Oof!
WHAP

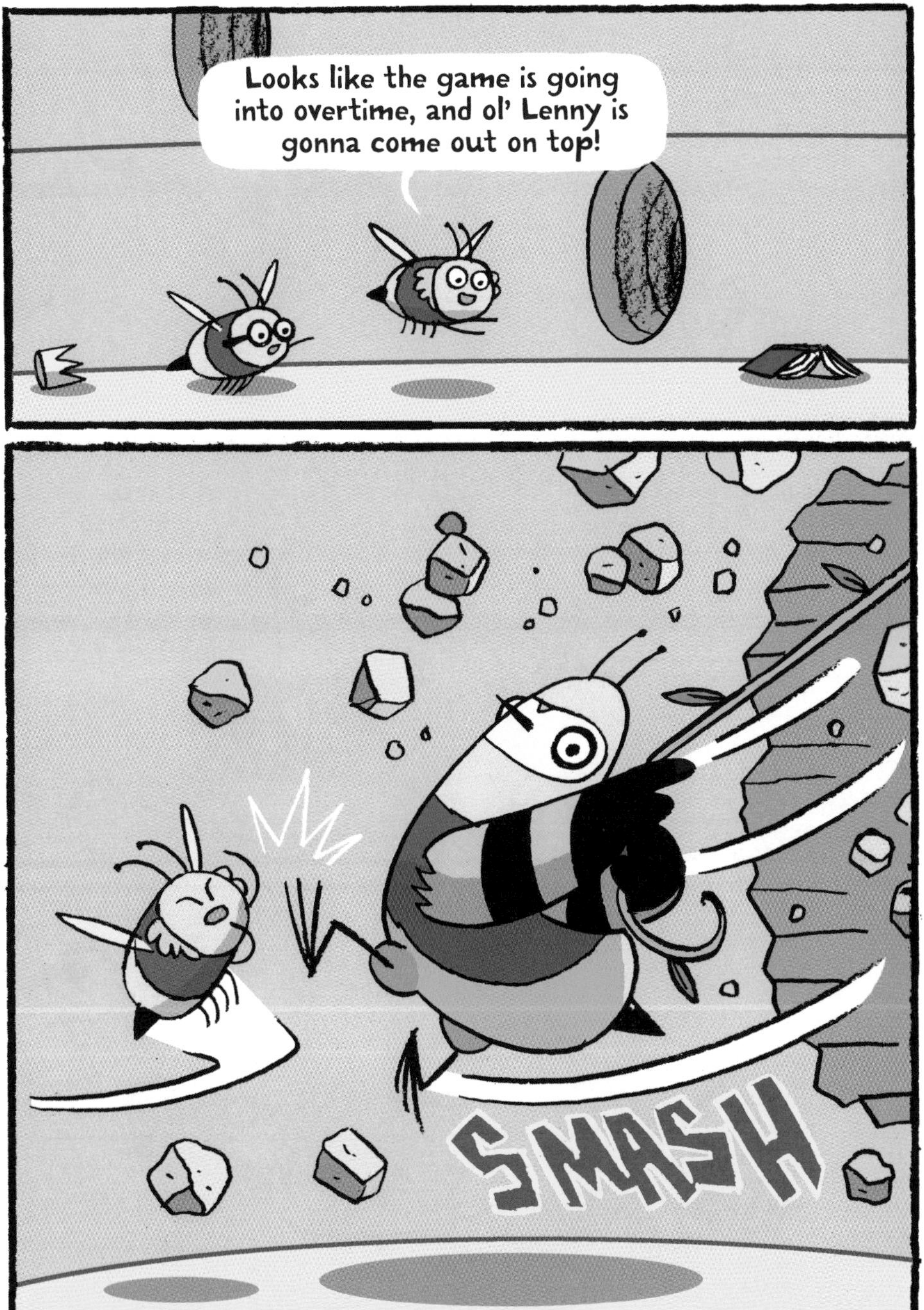
Looks like the game is going into overtime, and ol' Lenny is gonna come out on top!
SMASH

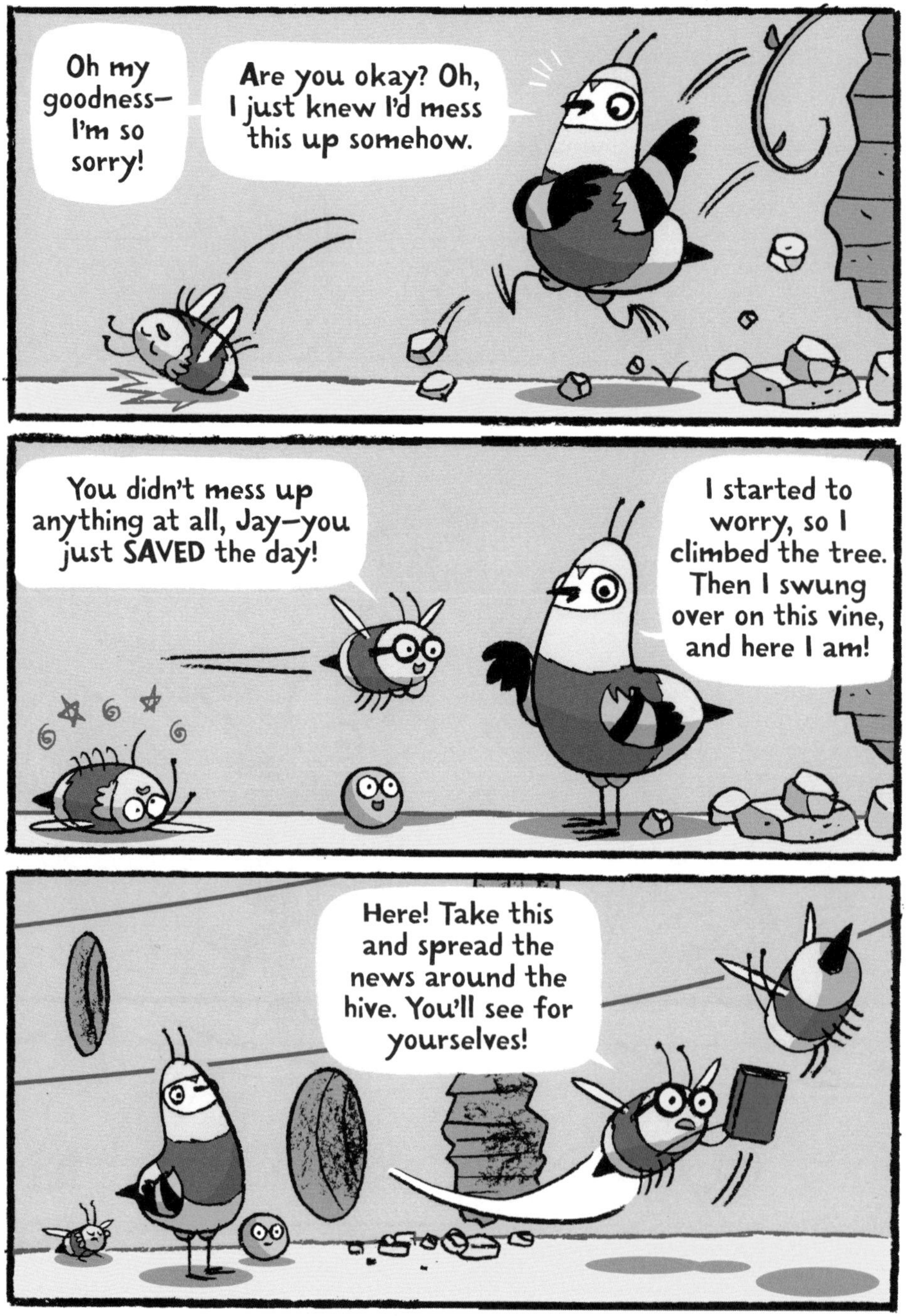
Oh my goodness—I'm so sorry!
Are you okay? Oh, I just knew I'd mess this up somehow.
You didn't mess up anything at all, Jay—you just SAVED the day!
I started to worry, so I climbed the tree. Then I swung over on this vine, and here I am!
Here! Take this and spread the news around the hive. You'll see for yourselves!

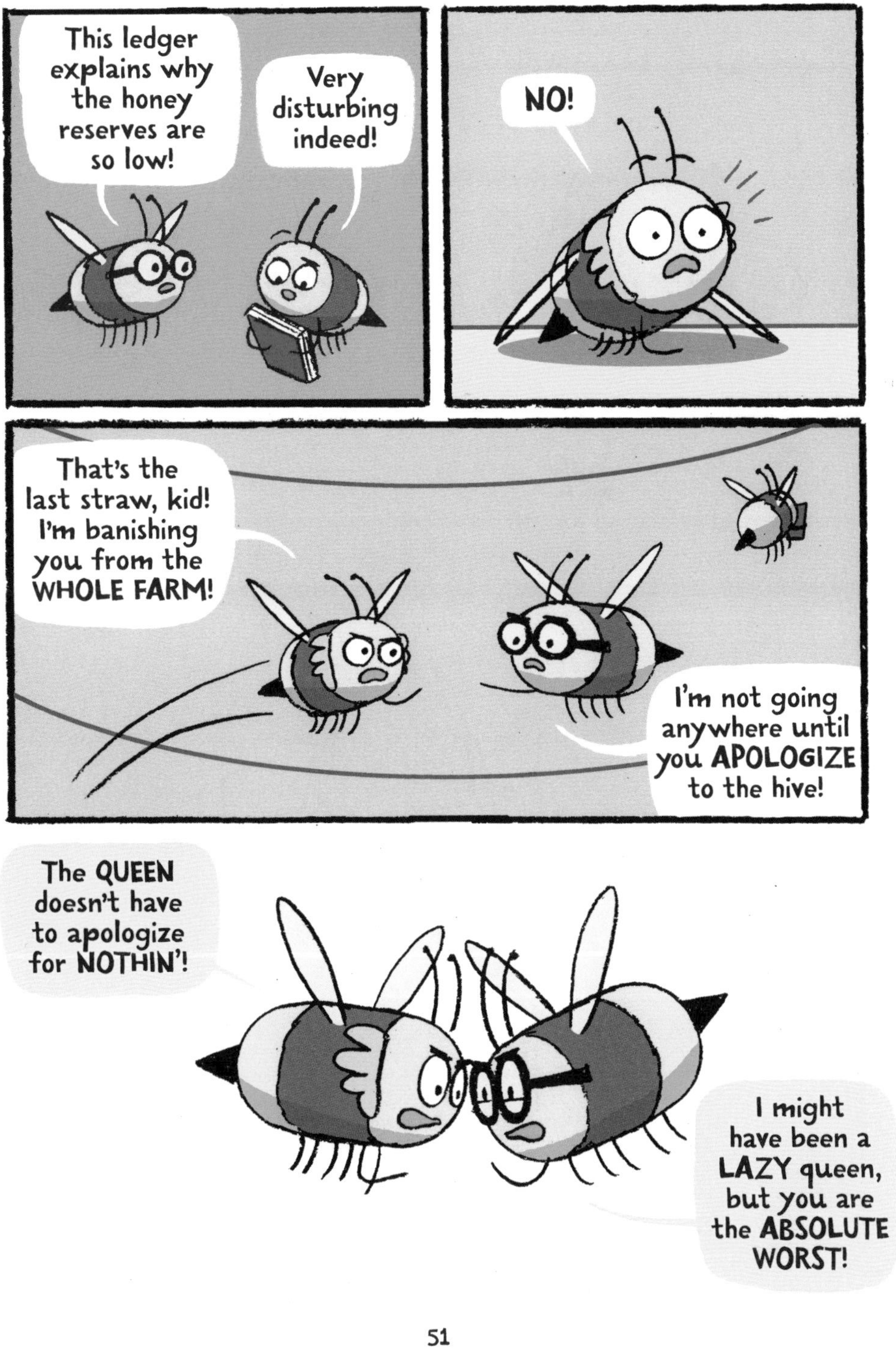
This ledger explains why the honey reserves are so low!
Very disturbing indeed!
NO!
That's the last straw, kid! I'm banishing you from the WHOLE FARM!
I'm not going anywhere until you APOLOGIZE to the hive!
The QUEEN doesn't have to apologize for NOTHIN'!
I might have been a LAZY queen, but you are the ABSOLUTE WORST!

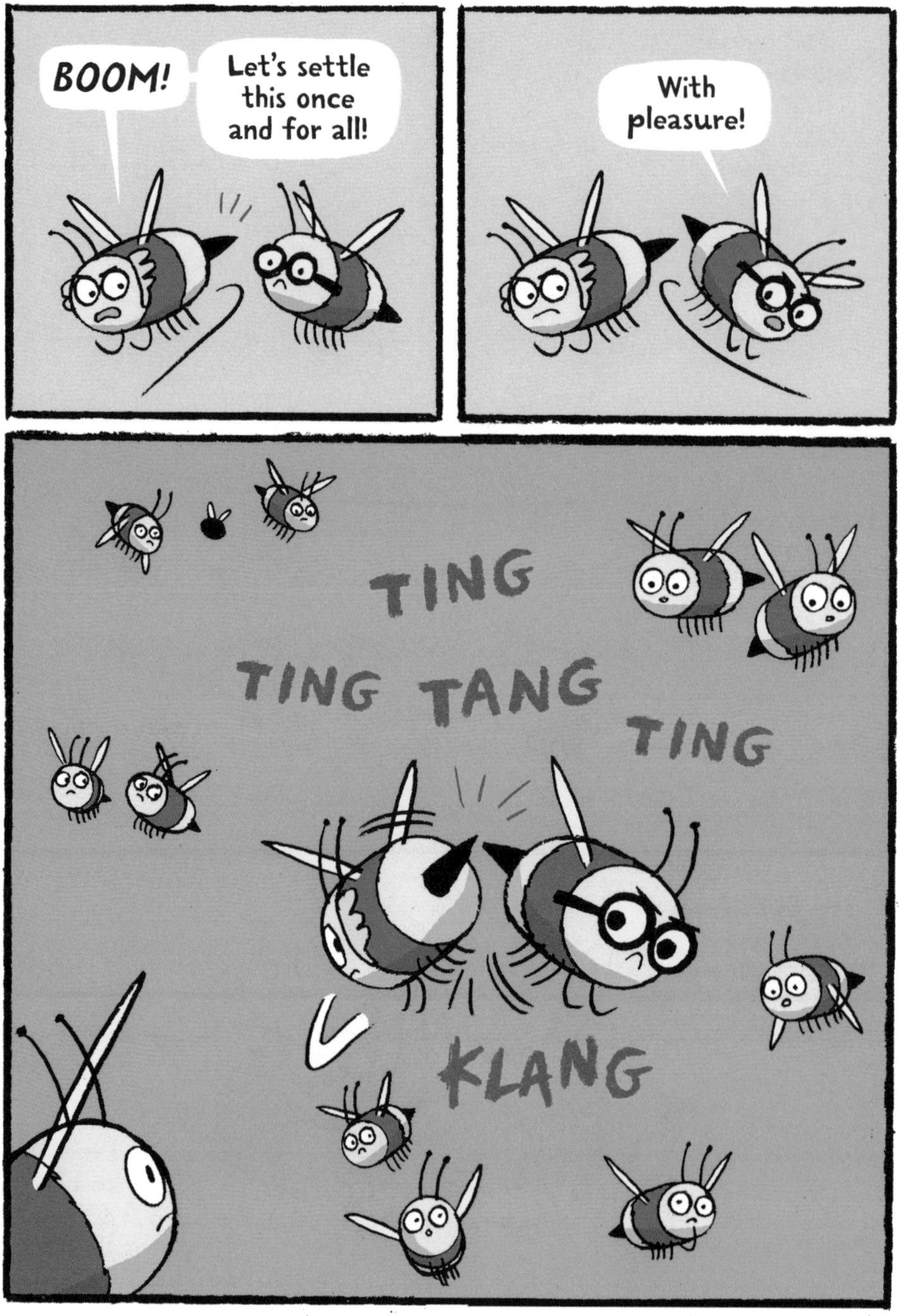
BOOM!
Let's settle this once and for all!
With pleasure!
TING
TING TANG
TING
KLANG

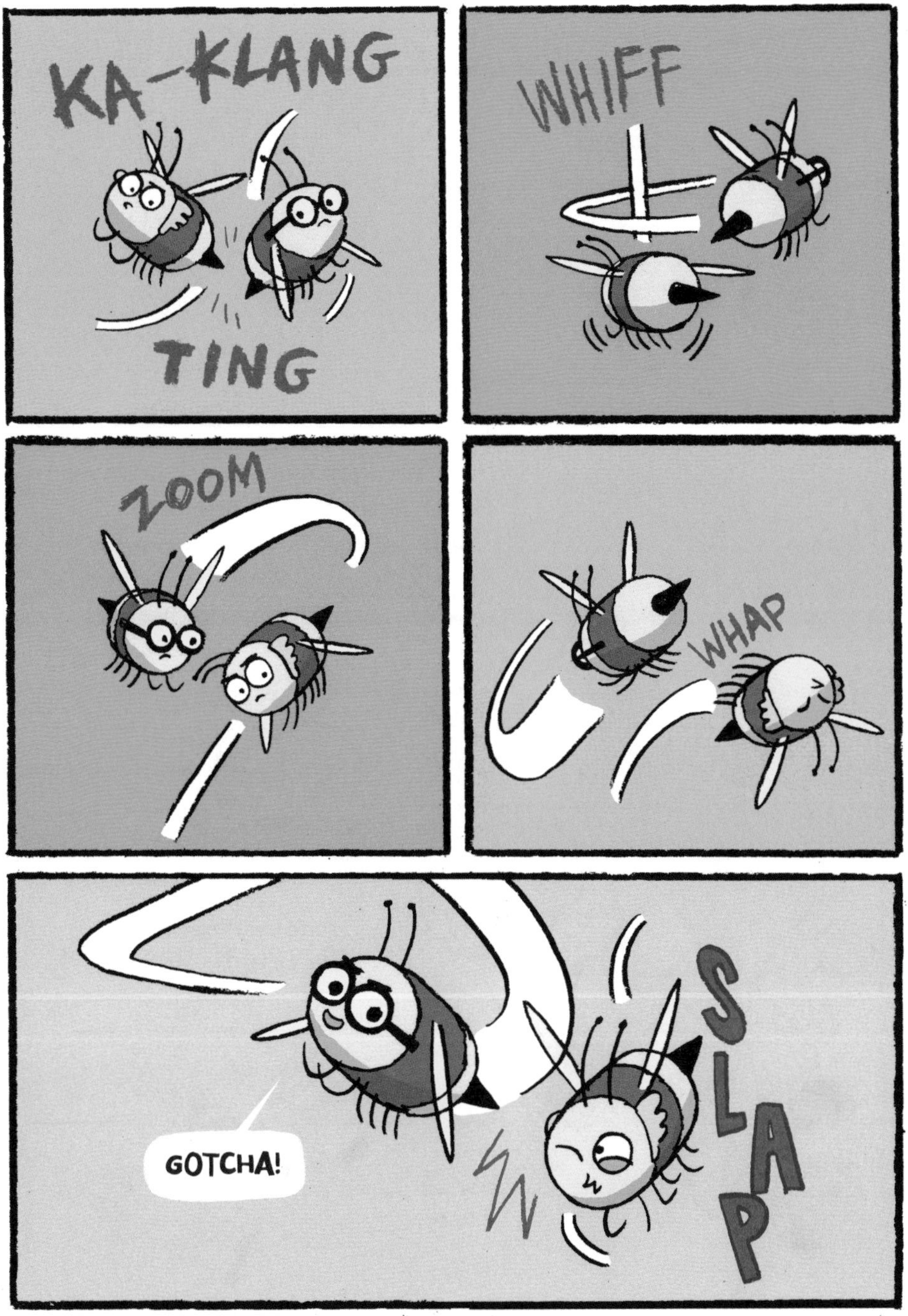
KA-KLANG
TING
WHIFF
ZOOM
WHAP
GOTCHA!
SLAP

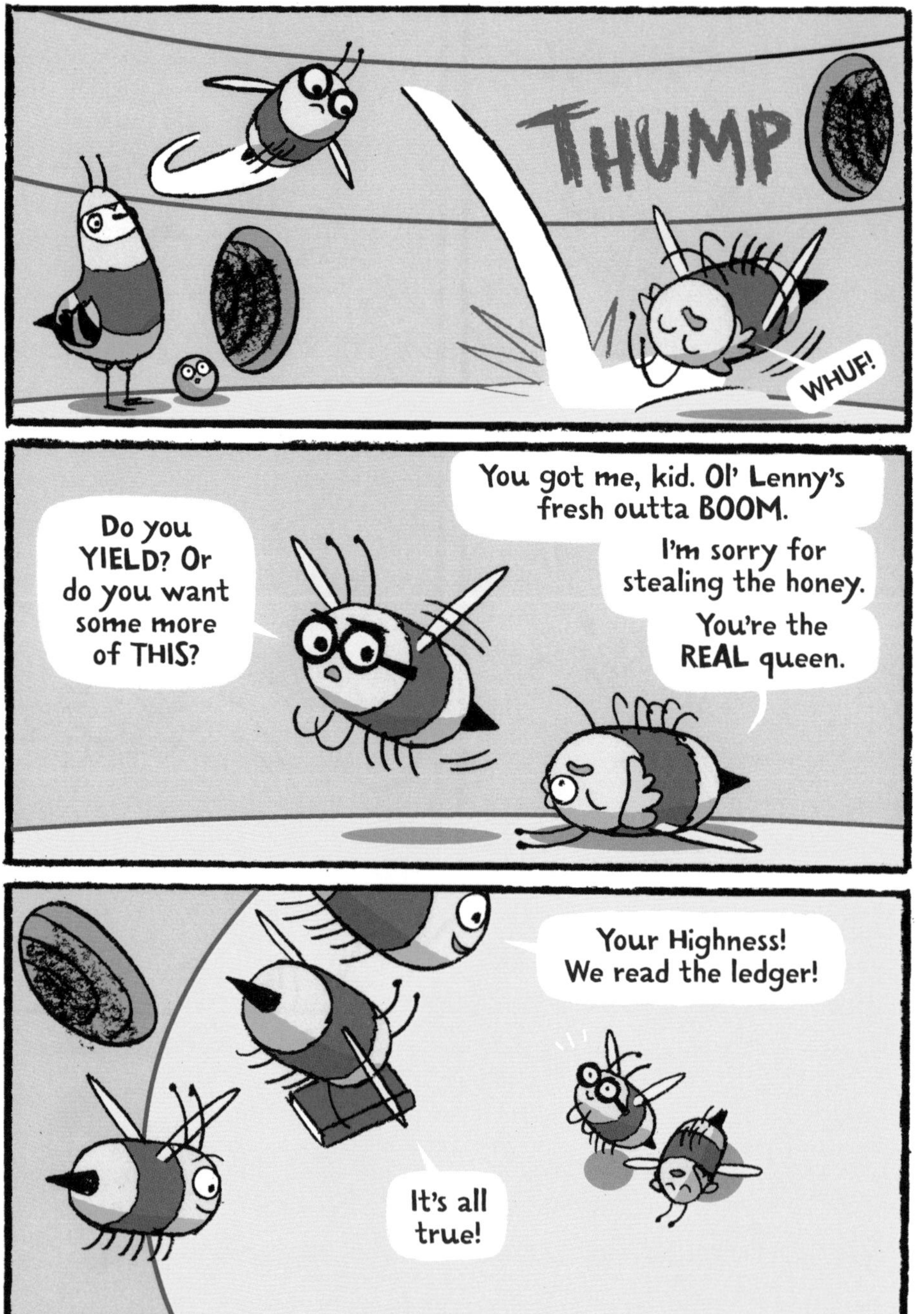
THUMP
WHUF!
Do you YIELD? Or do you want some more of THIS?
You got me, kid. Ol' Lenny's fresh outta BOOM.
I'm sorry for stealing the honey.
You're the REAL queen.
Your Highness! We read the ledger!
It's all true!

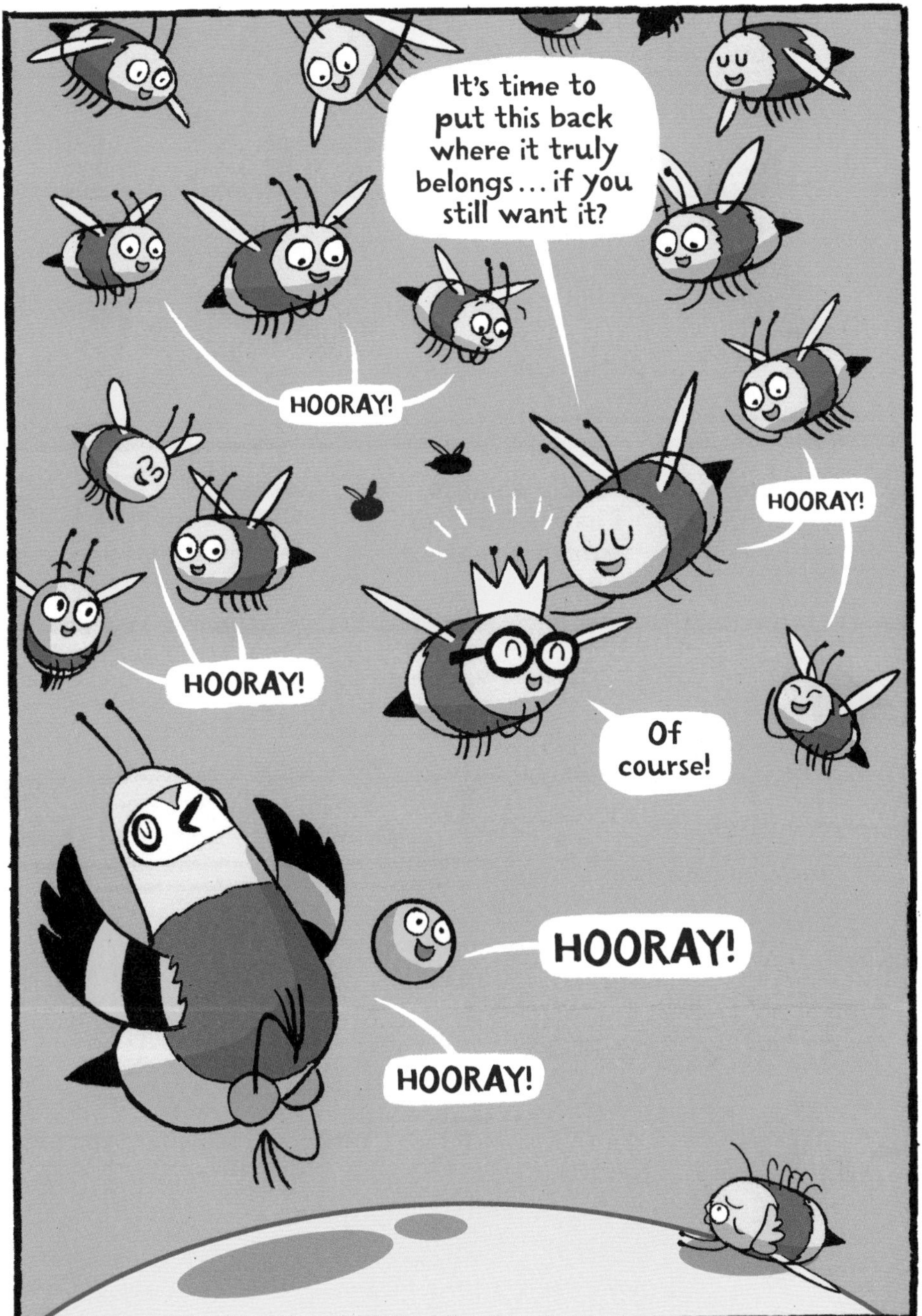
It's time to put this back where it truly belongs... if you still want it?
HOORAY!
HOORAY!
HOORAY!
Of course!
HOORAY!
HOORAY!

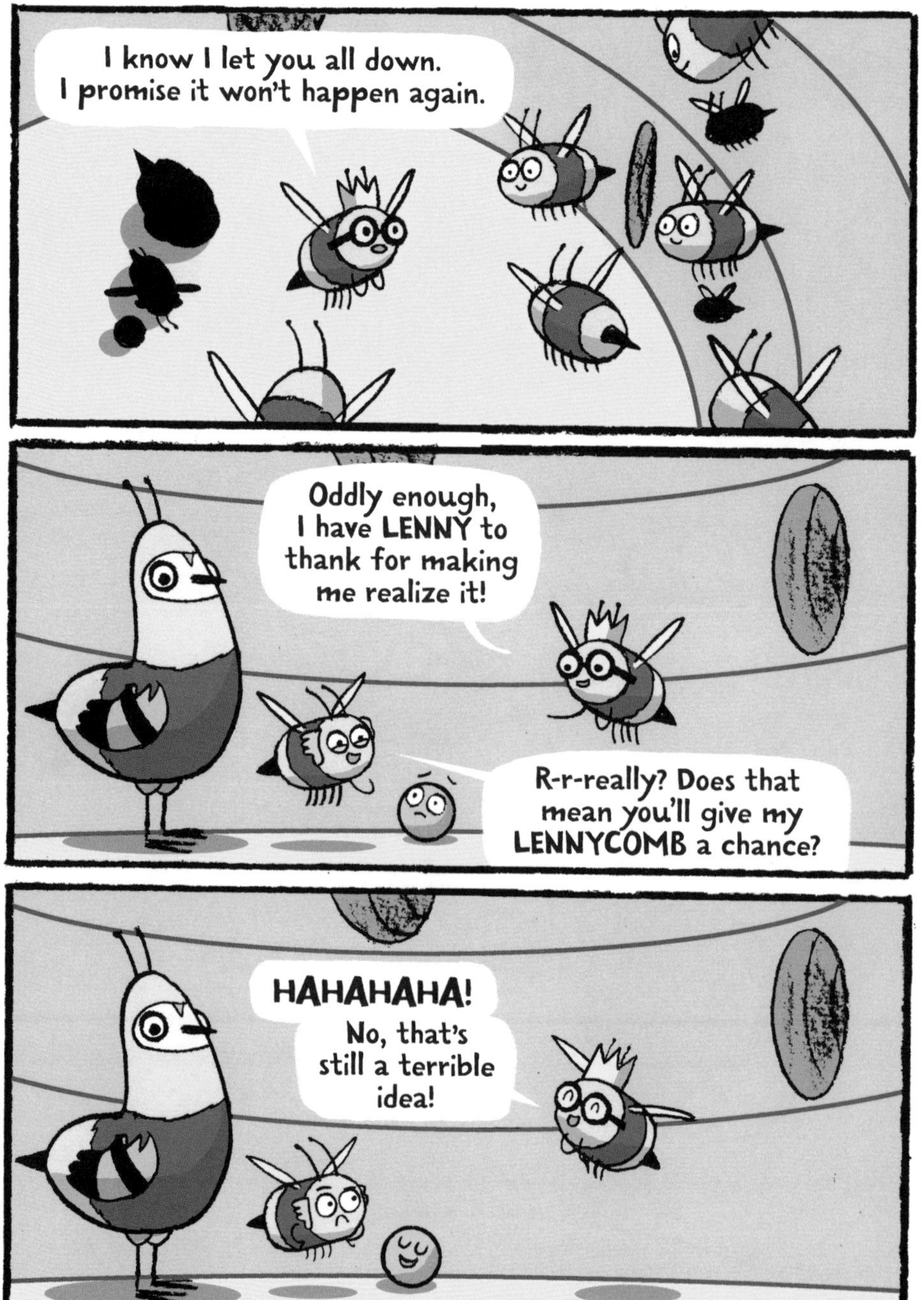
I know I let you all down. I promise it won't happen again.
Oddly enough, I have LENNY to thank for making me realize it!
R-r-really? Does that mean you'll give my LENNYCOMB a chance?
HAHAHAHA!
No, that's still a terrible idea!

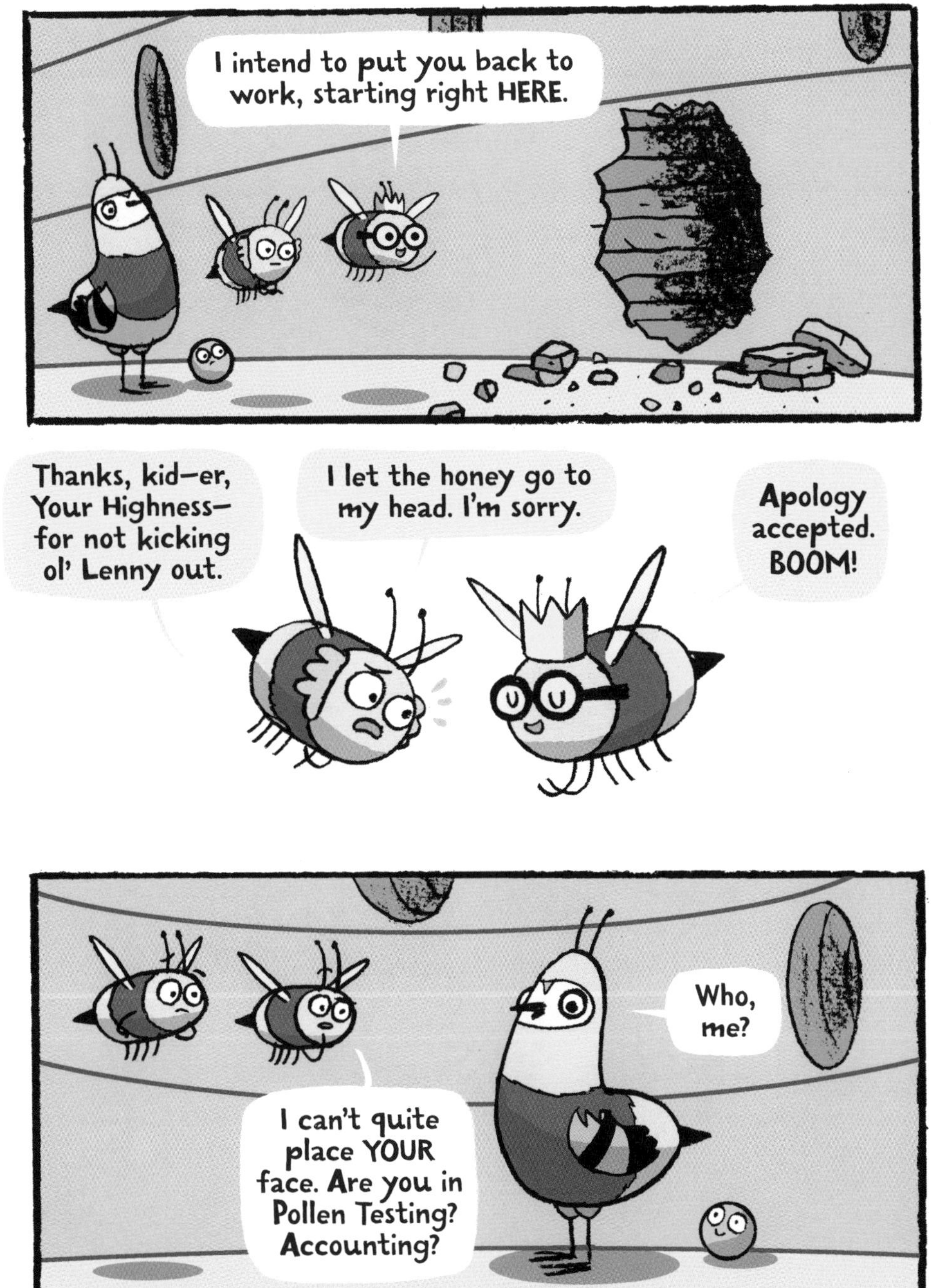
I intend to put you back to work, starting right HERE.
Thanks, kid—er, Your Highness—for not kicking ol' Lenny out.
I let the honey go to my head. I'm sorry.
Apology accepted. BOOM!
Who, me?
I can't quite place YOUR face. Are you in Pollen Testing? Accounting?

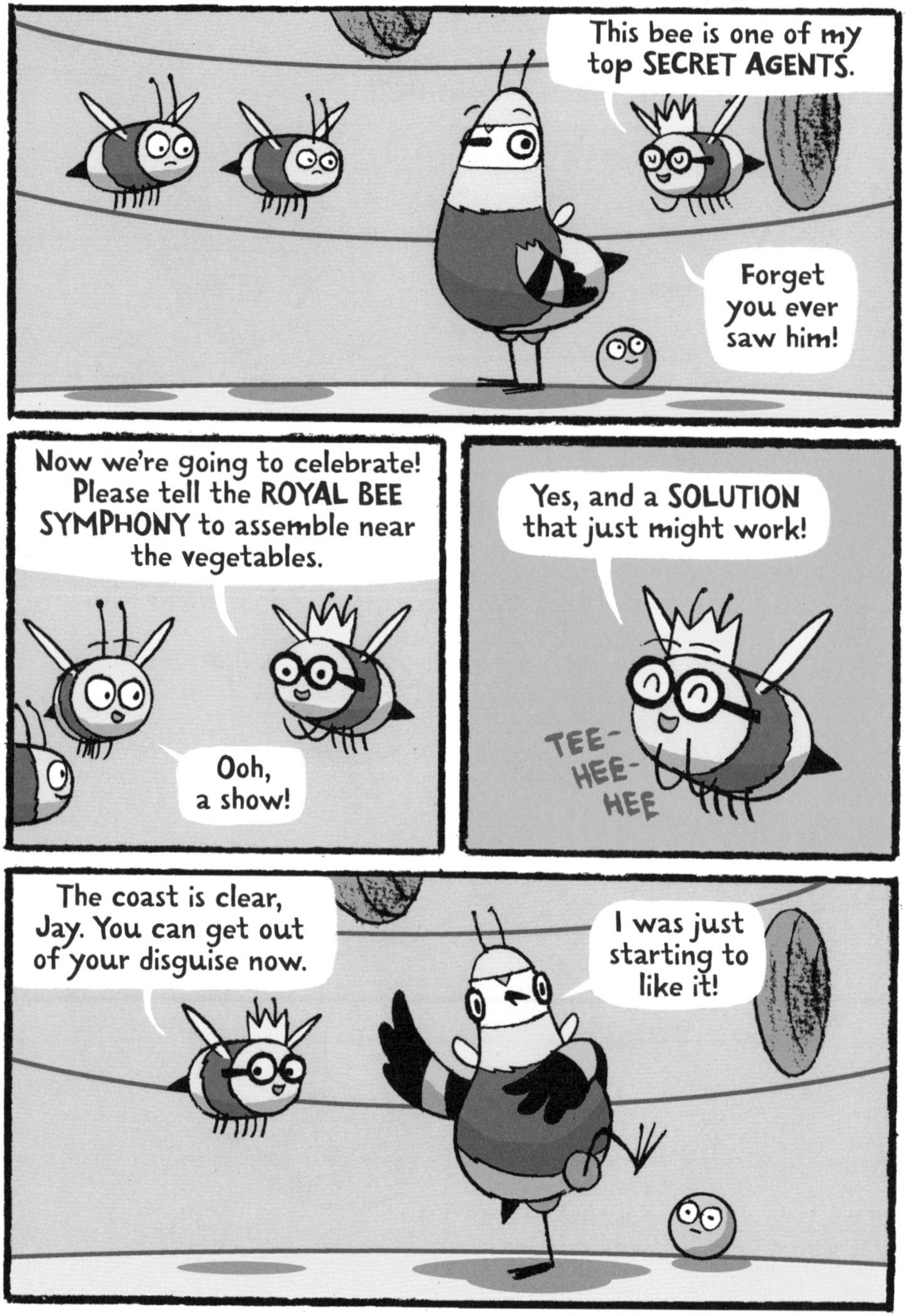
This bee is one of my top SECRET AGENTS.
Forget you ever saw him!
Now we're going to celebrate! Please tell the ROYAL BEE SYMPHONY to assemble near the vegetables.
Ooh, a show!
Yes, and a SOLUTION that just might work!
TEE-HEE-HEE
The coast is clear, Jay. You can get out of your disguise now.
I was just starting to like it!

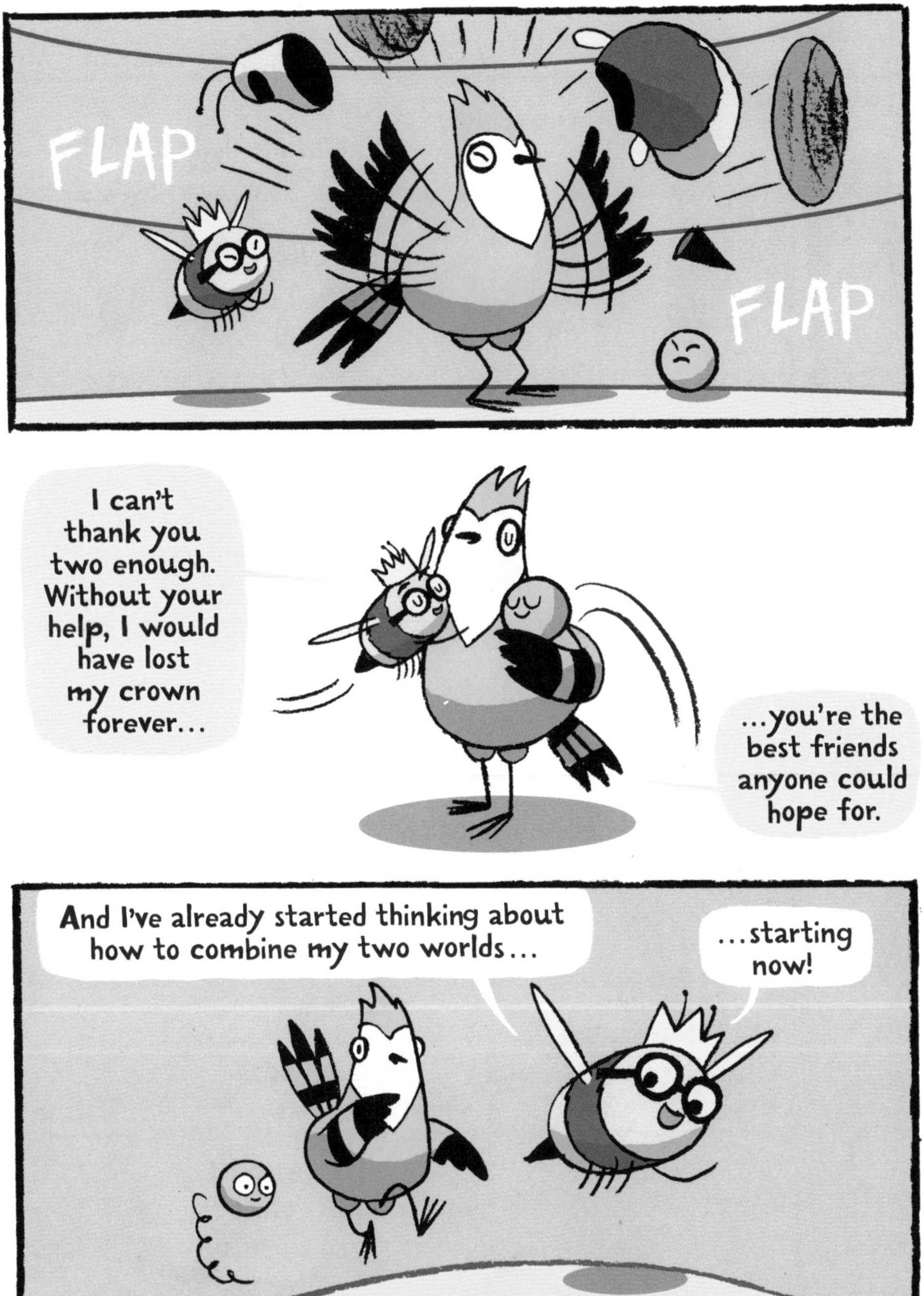
FLAP
FLAP
I can't thank you two enough. Without your help, I would have lost my crown forever...
...you're the best friends anyone could hope for.
And I've already started thinking about how to combine my two worlds...
...starting now!

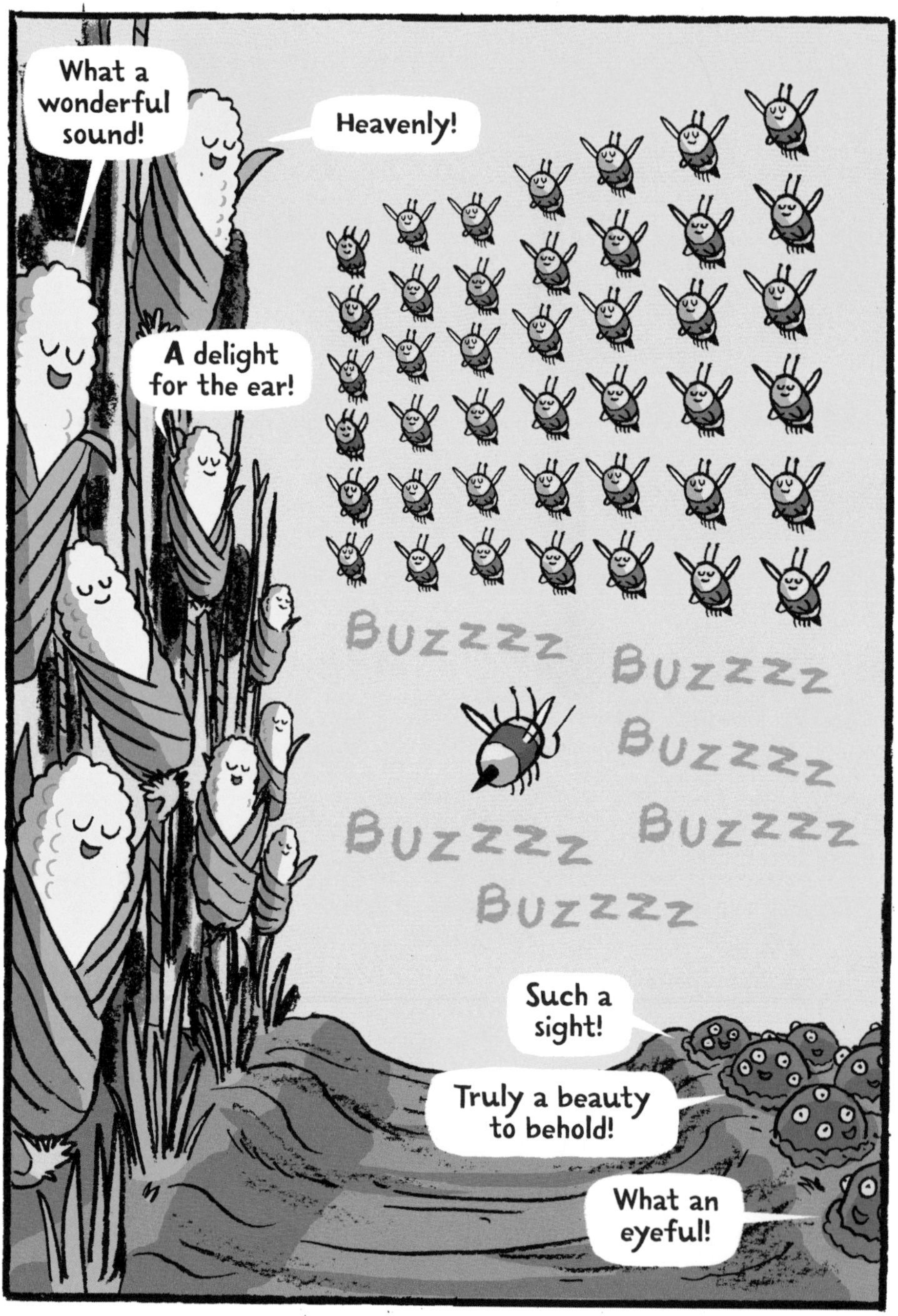
What a wonderful sound!
Heavenly!
A delight for the ear!
BUZZZZ
BUZZZZ
BUZZZZ
BUZZZZ
BUZZZZ
BUZZZZ
Such a sight!
Truly a beauty to behold!
What an eyeful!

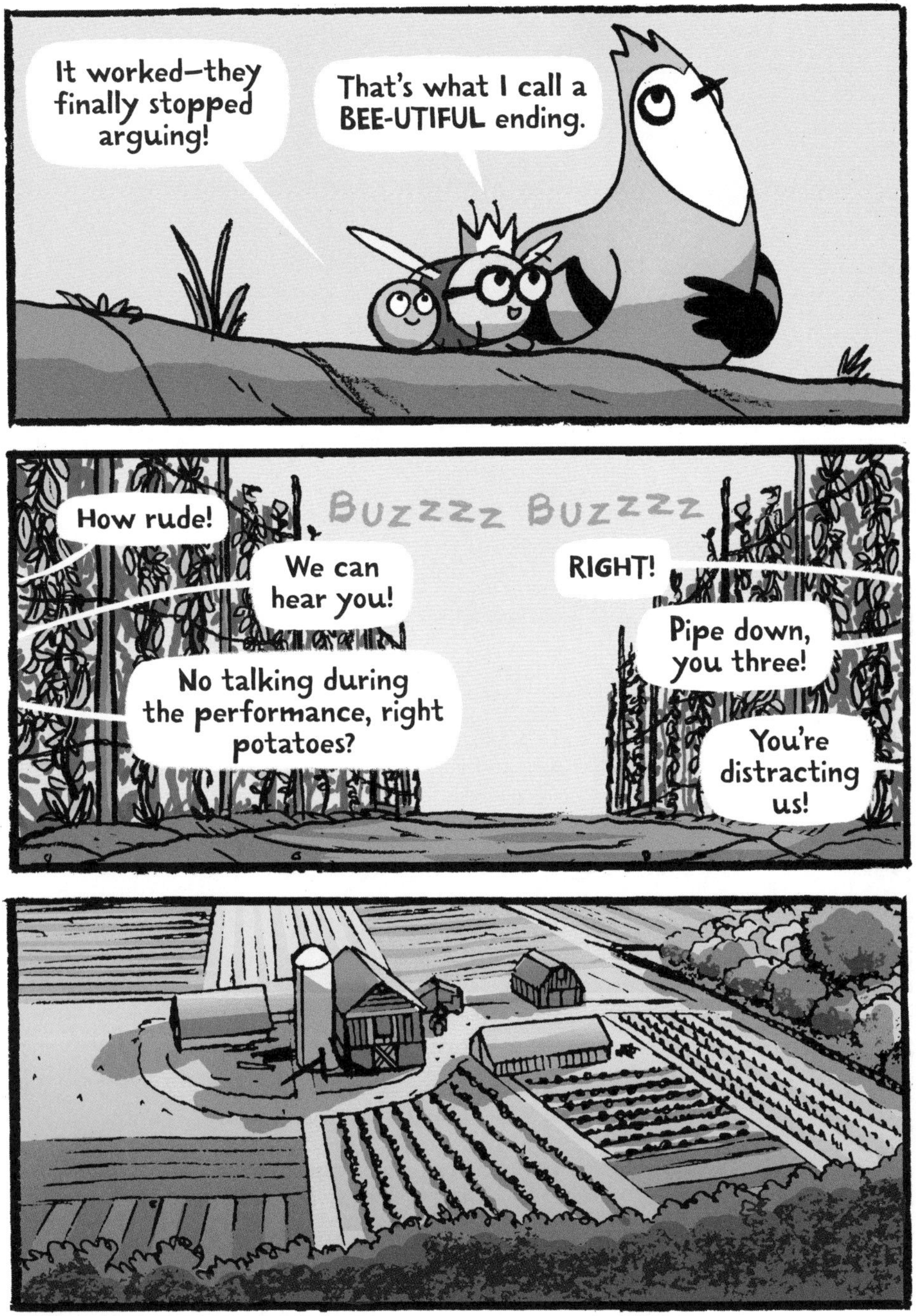
It worked—they finally stopped arguing!
That's what I call a **BEE-UTIFUL** ending.
BUZZZZ BUZZZZ
How rude!
We can hear you!
RIGHT!
Pipe down, you three!
No talking during the performance, right potatoes?
You're distracting us!

Thank you to Bret Parks, Juliet Parks, Elise Parks,
Robin Parks, and Ssalefish Comics, without whom
this book would not have been possible.

HarperAlley is an imprint of HarperCollins Publishers.

Pea, Bee, & Jay #2: Wannabees
Copyright © 2020 by Brian Smith
All rights reserved. Printed in Slovenia.
No part of this book may be used or reproduced in any manner whatsoever without written permission
except in the case of brief quotations embodied in critical articles and reviews. For information address
HarperCollins Children's Books, a division of HarperCollins Publishers, 195 Broadway, New York, NY 10007.
www.harperalley.com

Library of Congress Control Number: 2020931680
ISBN 978-0-06-298120-2 — ISBN 978-0-06-298119-6 (pbk.)

The artist used pencils, paper, a computer, and bee poop (lots and lots
of bee poop) to create the digital illustrations for this book.
Typography by Erica De Chavez and Andrew Arnold
20 21 22 23 24   GPS   10 9 8 7 6 5 4 3 2 1
❖
First Edition